I0673380

PRINTHOUSE BOOKS
PRESENTS

Unexpected Power
Fantasy & Supernatural

Brigitte Marshall
VIP INK Publishing Group, Inc.
Atlanta, GA.

Cover art designed by Teodora Chinde.
Editor: Shelby Oates

ISBN: 978-0-9965701-8-3

Library of Congress Cataloging-in-
Publication Data
#2015952710

1. Science Fiction 2. Romance
3. Fantasy & Supernatural 4.Brigitte
Marshall 5.LGBT

Printed in the United States of America

*Dedicated to my friends and family who
challenged me to go beyond what I thought
was possible, thanks for everything!*

A marketing analyst by day and superhero by night, Vita embraces her new life ... until she meets Toni, a beautiful woman who Vita falls hard for. Things are going well but when the police want to question Vita about a robbery witnesses say the superhero committed, she is determined to uncover the truth even if it means finding out truths that may cost her dearly .... her job, her reputation and most importantly ... her heart.

Table of Contents

THE STORM

Flipping slowly through the channels of the Monday morning news programs, Vita watched in disbelief at the destruction the three-minute tornado dealt on her city. Homes were destroyed, cars crushed by falling trees and massive flooding kept most roads deserted. There were five reported deaths; a mother and her two kids were killed when a falling tree crushed their car and two teenagers had been electrocuted when they stepped on a fallen live wire. And, both accidents happened less than five miles from where Vita spent the night.

"Ouch!" Vita moaned as she sat up putting her feet on the floor. *Too many vodka shots!* -- she thought to herself. The news stories kept coming: flooded cars, roofs ripped off, million dollar homes with no electricity and so much more.

Vita turned her attention back to the TV and that's when reality started coming back, memories of the night just before the storm which started out so sweetly. The partying, the dancing, the drinking and the sex!

Vita heard the forecasts warning a tornado would be moving into the city of Atlanta and surrounding cities with wind gusts of sixty to seventy miles per hour. Vita planned to go home after work and wait the storm out like everyone else. She wanted to be ready in case the forecast was right this time. Then she got the call from Simone.

As she shut off the TV, she remembered the best part of the night of that big storm: looking over at the woman sleeping on the other side of the bed in the hotel room. Long auburn hair covered one side of the pillow and she was naked underneath the covers that barely covered the lean, toned body. Her ass was showing a little and Vita had to stop herself from running her fingers down her white back and from softly kissing one of those smooth ass cheeks.

Simone was an amazing woman. She was five feet, seven inches tall and worked out five days a week to keep that Irish-heritage body tight. She was a beautiful thirty-two year old successful bankruptcy lawyer with a modern, posh office in the downtown area ... and ... married. Vita had met Simone at a fundraiser for a local children's charity. They exchanged numbers that night and had sex for the first time ten days later. Their friendship was uncomplicated— purely functional rather than emotional. They got together mostly when Simone's kids had a sleepover or were visiting

family and her husband was out of town.
Those nights usually consisted of dinner,
drinks, gossip, flirting and sex. Simone
always got a suite with a balcony and
spectacular view of the city at one of the
local hotels. They would sit on the
balcony for a while, chat about current
events and what was going on in their
lives and enjoy each other ... over and
over again. Since there was a big storm
brewing, Vita had not spent the night as
usual; instead she headed home just
around sunset.

Sipping some strong morning tea
to help chase out a massive hangover,
Vita thought about her life, friends and
lovers.

Raised in a two-parent home,
Vita grew up in a middle-class northeast
neighborhood. She was an only child
with lots of aunts, uncles and cousins.
Vita went to private school, played
sports, graduated with a 3.0 grade point
average and then went to college. It was
in college that she met Samantha. They
clicked immediately and became
inseparable. Samantha had a boyfriend
she'd been dating for nine months and
the relationship was physically abusive.
Vita tried to convince Samantha to
leave, telling her that all women
deserved better but no matter what she
said or how many times she said it, Sam
stayed with the jerk.

Unlike Vita, Sam didn't have any family. She grew up in foster care and went to college on an academic scholarship. She never really believed she could do better than the abusive guy who was the first and only person to show her love. And he really did, but it was always a cycle of temper and violence and then back to a show of love. One night six months ago, Vita got a call that Sam was in the hospital. Her boyfriend had beaten her so badly she was in a coma and possibly suffering from brain damage.

Visiting the hospital, standing over her friend's bed, Vita vowed she would do something to help others in Sam's position. At home that night, Vita pulled out a necklace Sam had given her years ago. It was a beautiful gold ankh. It was the one thing Sam had that belonged to her mother. Sam explained that the ankh was one of the most known symbols of ancient Egypt and to wear it as a symbol of power, virtue, wisdom and the key to freedom. Sam also told Vita that she remembered her mother saying that if you held it up to the stars and prayed really hard, the ankh could also be a reagent for a reincarnation spell -- a path, a bridge of the spirits and power.

Sam told Vita the ankh didn't work for her, so Vita could have it as a gift to remember her by. "If it was true, it would have worked for me and my life wouldn't be so fucked up."

So that night just before the storm hit, relaxed from the romp with Simone and thinking about her friend on a turbulent night, Vita walked up to the rooftop of her building. It was a beautiful night even though the forecast called for lightning and heavy thunderstorms. The sun made the far off storm cloud glow an odd purple color. Vita took the ankh out of its pouch and held it up to the sky with both hands. She began to pray for Sam to be healed, to wake up out of that six-month long coma and to leave her abusive relationship.

If only I could have been there for you Sam. I would have protected you. It started drizzling but Vita just stood there, holding the ankh up to the sky, just like Sam's mother had instructed her daughter so long ago. Lightning lit up the sky, but Vita stood her ground deep in thought and swirling with emotions. The rain came down heavier and heavier but Vita didn't move. A young modern woman, Vita realized she actually believed in the spirit and power of the ankh and the story Sam told. Sam hadn't really believed, she had been too busy just surviving the hard life that was thrown at her.

Vita had always felt spiritual, always felt a power surrounding people that they never tapped into. "Transform me! Change me!"

Vita thrust the shimmering ankh as high as her arms could reach, "I'll protect her!"

BOOM!!   CRACK!!!

A thunderous bolt of lightning knocked Vita to the ground. A ring of fire licked around her while a bolt of electricity ran through her entire body from head to toes rendering her unconscious.

When Vita awoke in the morning, the sun was just coming up. She opened her eyes fully and realized she was still on the roof. Her clothes were completely tattered and ripped to shreds. Her black hair was sticking up all over her head and her shoes had literally disintegrated. The last thing she remembered was praying with the ankh held high. She looked around for it but all she found was the little bag that had held it. *What the hell happened to me last night? Maybe I was robbed! But what did they do to my shoes and hair? No time for that now, I have to get ready for work.*

Back down in her apartment, Vita fell briefly asleep again. Then woke up with the TV on the local news. Dizzy and confused from the storm, the memories flooding through her mind and the sadness about the deaths from the tornado, Vita shook her head and tried to get back to the here and now.

She put on the radio, went into the bathroom and was about to step into a steaming shower when she saw it ... the ankh shape branded into her abdomen, right below her breasts covering all of her stomach, all the way down to her bellybutton!

Sitting in a meeting at work, Vita couldn't concentrate. She kept touching her stomach, sometimes scratching it like she had a rash or something.

"Vita, are you with us?" Vita looked around at her boss, noticing co-workers were staring at her. "Do you have the conversion numbers for the mobile ad campaigns?"

"Yep, right here. Sorry about that!" Vita gave her weekly performance report of all the campaigns she was working on but she couldn't stop thinking about the ankh burning a hole in her stomach!

As marketing analyst in the mobile division at the ad agency, Vita was responsible for tracking the performance of multiple mobile ad campaigns for five national car rental companies. She was personable and on the fast track at her job. She was thorough, detailed and worked late when needed, making it known that she was aiming for the VP position of the mobile ad division.

At seven that evening Vita finally left the office. She couldn't believe nine hours had passed because she couldn't remember most of what went on all day. She called the hospital and checked on Sam. "No change Vita," the nurse reported.

It was six short blocks to the subway station but Vita decided to walk another five to the next station. With a buzzing brain and a restless feeling, some exercise was needed to work off the building energy. How was she going to explain the oversized ankh on her body to her friends and most especially the friends with benefits? She didn't have any tattoos and still only had one hole in each of her ears for earrings. *Why is it there, will it go away?* - - were thoughts that kept circling around in her

mind. It didn't hurt but just the fact that
it was there made Vita uncomfortable,
nauseous even. Walking down the street
she felt like everyone was staring at her,
like they all knew the ankh was there
under her shirt and could see it.

She stopped at a crosswalk and
waited with the rest of the crowd. Her
mind raced as she scanned the people.
As the crowd in front of her started to
cross, Vita followed. She took one step
into the street and before she got the
other foot down a car raced by, plowing
into the group in front of her. Vita froze!
Everything was happening in slow
motion. Two men were trapped
underneath the car that ran into the
crowd and she saw the driver slumped
over the steering wheel. People were
screaming, some were taking videos and
pictures with their cell phones and blood
was everywhere!

Vita's stomach was on fire, like
the ankh was burning a hole in her gut!
All of a sudden, in a robotic-like state,
Vita found she was walking over to the
car, lifting it up with one hand and
pulling the two men out from
underneath. Gently she lowered the car,
ripped off the driver's side door and
pulled out the woman driver. She lined
all three up alongside each other and
began CPR. Vita lowered her lips onto
the first man and with only two breaths

the man was revived and moaning as he struggled to get his bearings and figure out what just happened. She repeated the actions on the other two victims and they all sputtered back to life quickly under her care.

A crowd gathered and people were cheering and clapping. Vita panicked as she saw all the cell phones taking pictures and videos of her. She could hear the police and ambulance sirens getting closer and an overwhelming desire to get out of there fast came over her. But there was no way to get out. The crowd had encircled her and was getting closer and closer. Sweat starting forming on Vita's hands and face and the burn in her stomach was almost unbearable. The crowd drew closer and closer. They wanted to touch her, to feel this superwoman. All of a sudden, without warning, Vita was airborne. She was flying above the crowd, ascending higher and higher until she was flying as high as some of the tallest buildings in the city. She landed on the rooftop of her own building in the same spot where she woke up with the ankh burned in her stomach that morning.

As she had taken flight, both fear and fantasy raced through her mind. She thought of superhero clothes and as she did, her own clothes were replaced with

the outfit she envisioned. Black lycra
pants that fit like a glove, a skin-tight
black and purple top with a purple
design on the long sleeves. She looked
down at her feet and her shoes were
gone and she was wearing black boots
with wings on the side. Surprisingly,
they were nice and comfortable even
with the high heel. The only thing on her
that was the same was her long hair. Her
friends always told Vita that her hair
was one of her best features. She had
been blessed with long, thick, naturally
curly hair. As a child she wore it in
pigtails, in college she cut it off and went
with a close boy cut with a V at the nape
of the neck, and as an adult she got it
relaxed every six months to straighten it
out and wore it straight or in a curly afro
type style. Vita's parents were both
African American but she had inherited
the hair of the Native American heritage
from her mother's side of the family.
Her hair was naturally black but she
spent so much time in the sun that it
brought out some natural bright tones
making it appear she had it highlighted.

Once in her apartment, Vita
turned on the television. She flipped
from one news channel to the next and
the accident was on every local channel;
soon it even showed up on CNN. She
watched in awe at the pictures of her
lifting the car, pulling off the door

handle, giving CPR and flying off. She started recording CNN because she couldn't believe what she was seeing.

Three thousand miles away in Los Angeles, CA, Vita's old friend Kristen Moore was also watching the news and taping it. She couldn't shake the feeling that the superhero looked a lot like the woman who broke her heart: Vita. Same height, same build, same long, silky black hair. *But how*, Kristen thought. *How did she do that?* There was only one way to find out!

THE PAST

Kristen and Vita met three years ago in Chicago when they both worked for a small ad agency. Kristen was the manager and Vita was hired on as a marketing analyst. The company only had eight employees and was housed in the old Sears building in downtown Chicago. Vita was new to the area so Kristen invited her to lunch often. They soon became friends, meeting for drinks and dinner after work, hanging out on weekends, going to art gallery openings and open houses on homes they couldn't possibly afford yet. Kristen invited Vita to her apartment and cooked her dinner several times. Cooking was one of Kristen's passions and she was always willing to prepare a home cooked meal for friends.

At Vita's six-month anniversary with the company, Kristen invited her over for a special celebratory Saturday night dinner. And Kristen went all out! She cleaned the apartment from top to bottom, bought fresh flowers and even bought a new outfit for the occasion. Vita wasn't arriving until eight, all preparations were done by six giving Kristen plenty of time for a long hot bath. She lit the candles surrounding her claw footed tub and climbed in.

Everything was perfect including a nice bottle of champagne on ice in the fridge. She was cooking one of Vita's favorite meals: honey glazed salmon, fresh string beans and homemade mashed potatoes. Kristen recalled the first time she made that meal for Vita, the way her eyes lit up as she took her first bite, the way her lips moved as she chewed. After eating everything on the plate that night, Vita smiled from ear to ear. Kristen noticed how beautiful that smile was. Her teeth were pearly white and at that moment, Kristen thought she was the most beautiful woman she had ever seen. Vita was tall, her skin a lovely chocolate-caramel color with a reddish tint to it. But the most striking feature was her hair—long, thick, soft and silky. Kristen loved the way it bounced when Vita walked or the way it blew all over the place when the wind hit it. More than once she had imagined running her hands through it as they kissed. Kristen had never shared with Vita that she was a lesbian but she had a suspicion Vita knew. Once when they first met, Vita asked Kristen if she had a boyfriend or was dating anyone. Kristen's response was short, "I date." End of discussion.

Vita never brought it up again. Kristen decided that until she told Vita about her sexual preferences, she would keep her far away from her gay friends and the clubs where they hung out just in case that would be a turn off to the lovely dark haired woman. But Kristen constantly daydreamed of walking into Fusion, the largest lesbian club on Chicago's north side, with Vita by her side. She longed to see the envy and jealousy in everyone's eyes as they walked hand-in-hand through the crowds. She imagined them standing side-by-side, Kristen's hand on the small of Vita's back, slowly making its way down and caressing that perfect ass. Vita lived up to her lively name in every part of her caramel body.

Kristen was a little shorter than Vita. She stood five foot six to Vita's tall five foot nine frame. Kristen had long legs but a short torso, small waist, hips she thought were too wide and perfect breasts. People thought Kristen was cute, even attractive in her own way but she had never been called pretty. She wasn't a natural beauty like Vita. But what she lacked due to genetics she made up with in fierce makeup, a tight hairdo worn in a natural healthy small afro style and expensive clothes, jewelry and shoes. Over the years Kristen had done very well at work, being promoted three times in five years to her current position as Senior VP of Sales at Lexicon Marketing Partners which afforded her a nice apartment and lifestyle.

On this special night Vita arrived right on time. Eight o'clock sharp. "You look beautiful," Vita said to her host as she entered the luxury apartment. She handed over a bottle of Rosé; her favorite champagne picked up on the way.

"Thanks," Kristen said. "The more the merrier. I've already got a bottle chilling." They walked into the kitchen and Vita sat at the island on one of the barstools as Kristen poured. "Try these," Kristen said as she pushed a small plate of appetizers in front of her guest.

"Yummy," Vita said as she grabbed one of the grilled shrimp and citrus skewers off the plate. "These are really, really good!"

"Glad you like them," smiled Kristen. "Got the recipe from a little food magazine I picked up last week." Kristen handed Vita a flute of champagne.

"Cheers!" They both said as they clicked glasses.

"Here's to a great six months of friendship," Kristen said and then they both took a sip.

Pandora was playing through Kristen's iPad and coming from tiny wireless speakers she had throughout the apartment. Kristen had set the table on her patio, so they moved out there for dinner. They ate, talked, drank, laughed and drank and laughed some more.

"We've finished off the second bottle already," Kristen yelled from the kitchen. "Want me to open another bottle?"

"Why not?" Vita yelled back. She was having a great time. It was a beautiful summer night. The food was good, the company was good and she was looking at one of the most amazing views of the Chicago skyline from the balcony where she sat.

After a while they moved inside, full from the great dinner and definitely drunk from the champagne. Every time a good song came on they both got up and danced. Casual dancing turned into close dancing, holding each other around the waist playfully putting their thighs between each other's thighs as they got low, low and lower. At one point they got so low that Kristen fell on top of Vita. They both started laughing in a heap on the floor. They tried to get up but fell back because they were so drunk. The second time Vita tried to get up, Kristen gently pushed her back down. Their eyes locked and the laughter was replaced with serious soul-searching looks.

Sensing where this was going, Vita was turned on and scared at the same time. She had never been with another woman before even though she had thought about it. She had only dated guys in the past and had just gotten out of a relationship with a co-worker two months ago. Vita really like him and thought the relationship was going somewhere but broke up with him when she found out he was cheating on her.

Kristen slowly got on top of Vita, putting her thigh between Vita's legs. She looked directly into Vita's eyes as they lay on the floor and slowly she lowered her face and kissed her full on the lips. When Vita didn't resist, Kristen kissed her harder, opening her mouth a little and sliding her tongue inside of Vita's mouth. Vita responded and began kissing Kristen with the same hunger and passion. They kissed for a few minutes and slowly started grinding on each other. When the dark haired beauty wrapped her hands around Kristen's neck and crushed their lips together, there was no doubt where the night was going to end up.

Kristen slipped her hand under Vita's shirt, now bold knowing her advances were wanted. She lifted the shirt and bra up and kissed each of Vita's breasts. Then she unzipped Vita's pants, pulled them down and took one of her legs out. She lifted her own dress, pulled her panties to the side and pressed her clit against Vita's bare leg.

They kissed and slowly grinded, moving until they were on each other clit to clit. After only a minute of this, Kristen felt herself starting to come. She tried to slow down but couldn't. Vita grabbed her ass, pulling her new lover harder into her body.

They were both moaning and grinding in unison, kissing each other, their clits hard, their asses moving up and down. After a few more seconds, Kristen came. "Oh shit, oh shit! I'm coming!" Her body jerked as she came all over Vita's thigh.

"Don't stop, please don't stop," Vita moaned. Kristen kept going, grinding on Vita's clit harder with more direct movements. "Yeah, right there," Vita said softly. "Right there!"

Kristen started grinding harder and faster. Vita grabbed her by the hair, nestled her face into Kristen's neck and moaned out loud as she came. Kristen could see goose bumps form on her breasts as her nipples got hard. Kristen then felt between Vita's legs and rubbed the slick come between her fingers like she was checking to see if she faked it. Vita felt what Kristen just did. *Strange*, she thought but was too relaxed and distracted to say anything.

"I think I better go," Vita said still lying underneath Kristen. Kristen got up and stood in the middle of the living room. Vita stood and pulled up her pants. The moment was very awkward since they had not eased into a physical relationship.

"Are you sure you're ok to drive?" Kristen asked.

"Yeah, I'm fine."

"Are you sure? You're welcome to stay here tonight if you want." Kristen desperately wanted Vita to stay, to spend the night. She envisioned them making love again and holding each other through the night.

"No, I'm fine, really," Vita said for a third time. All she wanted to do was get out of there so she could process what just happened. "I'll text you when I get home and we can talk tomorrow. Ok?" And with that Vita grabbed her bag, thanked Kristen for a wonderful dinner and left. Kristen tried to kiss her on the lips when they hugged but Vita turned away.

Not good, Kristen thought. *Not good.*

Things were never the same between them after that first sexual encounter. Vita got another job and left the company a few weeks later and she was always busy when Kristen did get through to her and tried to ask her out.

One Sunday morning Kristen went to the coffee house she knew Vita visited on most Sundays. She walked in and saw her sitting in the back at a small table reading the New York Times. Kristen hadn't been able to think of anything but their night together. She was in love with Vita and wanted to know what went wrong and how she could fix it. Vita didn't see Kristen until she was standing in front of her.

"Hi," Kristen said softly. "I hope I'm not bothering you."

Vita was startled. "No, no you're not bothering me. I'm just surprised to see you here. That's all. Have a seat." *May as well get this over with.*

Kristen started, "I just wanted to know what I did wrong, why you stopped talking to me. You responded to my kiss and the love making so I thought everything was ok."

Vita could see tears about to fall onto Kristen's cheeks and looked away. After an awkward silence, Vita said, "I did like it, I really did. I didn't want to lead you on thinking it was going to be more than what it was, just a one night thing. I just didn't know how to tell you." Vita felt terrible. This is what she had been avoiding all these months. This feeling right here! The look on Kristen's face made Vita wish she could take it back. "It's not that I don't like you Kristen. I've been attracted to women my whole life I think. I just didn't know you were too and that night at your

Brigitte Marshall

house, it just caught me off guard. I think you're great, a really nice person, a great friend but I'm just not attracted to you like that. I can't make the feelings come, it was a great night of really good sex, but I didn't want to lead you on knowing it wasn't going anywhere." *There, I said it.* It was off her chest.

Kristen was stunned. She had never been rejected before. She left without another word.

Things had been going well for Vita since that Sunday encounter with Kristen. She had a new job she really liked, was making new friends and had a clear conscience. Vita always felt that honesty was the best policy and it was best to tell the truth even if someone got hurt. She knew she had hurt Kristen but it was best to be honest, put it all behind them both. And that was what she was doing. After all, a person couldn't *MAKE* feelings just happen, so it was best to move on and not waste both of their time.

Vita went out that night to blow off some steam but had to cut the party short. "Hey you guys. I'm about to leave. I've got an early day tomorrow, meeting with the big boss at nine o'clock sharp," Vita yelled to her friends hoping they could hear something over the loud music blaring at the club. Nobody was paying any attention to her. Finally she

27

tapped one of her friend's shoulders and told her she was leaving. Vita walked out to her car, jumped in and took off.

"What the fuck! Don't tell me I have a flat tire! Not tonight!" She pulled over into an empty parking lot, got out of the car and walked around to the passenger side and there it was. A flat tire! "Fuck!" She screamed feeling way too tired to want to deal with this. Luckily she had AAA and called in for help. She gave them the address and walked back into the club. She found her friends, Kim and Alexandria, told them what happened and they waited with her outside. AAA was there in an hour and put on a spare tire.

"These are brand new tires," Vita complained to her friends. "They're less than two months old. I hope I can get the hole patched."

Vita took her car to the Goodyear repair shop near her office on Saturday morning. She was driving a 2002 Honda Civic with 120,000 miles on it. It was a good reliable car and she loved it but she was the only one. Her friends hated it and would only ride in it when absolutely necessary. The air conditioning didn't work well, the passenger window was off the track, the passenger seat was ripped on the side and the windshield was cracked. Not to mention all the weird sounds the car made when it was going down the road. She couldn't afford a new car on her salary but she could keep this one serviced and keep good tires on it.

After two hours the repairman walked into the bare waiting room. Her car was ready. "You may want to know that we didn't find a nail in your tire but found these." The serviceman held up two razors. "These were stuck into your tire."

Vita couldn't hide the shocked look on her face. "Thank you," she said to the mechanic as she paid him and left in a confused state of mind.

By the time Vita got home she couldn't even remember driving home. She didn't remember making any turns and there was no recollection of stopping at any lights or stop signs. She was completely shook up. *Who would put razors in my tires?*

Vita tried to put the tire incident behind her and chalked it up to random urban vandalism. A few weeks later she met some of her old friends out to celebrate Kim's fortieth birthday. They went to Diablo's, a new tapas restaurant in the heart of downtown Chicago where happy hour started at six o'clock. It was nice to be among friends again.

"We should do this more often," Vita said to them all, holding up her drink to toast. Everyone was feeling good and no one wanted the party to end.

"Let's go dancing," Alexandria yelled. They all looked at each other, sighed, laughed and then headed out to a dance club to dance off their dinner.

Two blocks from Diablo's was a boy bar that played old soul, R&B and house music. The girls were dancing as they walked through the doors. They headed straight for the dance floor and joined some half-naked boys, rubbing their clothed bodies against the almost bare bodies of the guys. The music was so loud and it was so hot, but it all felt so damn good. Vita was sandwiched between two guys who were wearing tight wrestling uniforms, their chest and legs out, their sweaty muscles flexing with each move.

Suddenly Vita felt a sharp blow to her head like she had been punched or hit with a heavy object. The punch was so hard it made her knees buckle and almost knocked her off her feet. She gathered herself, stood up straight and looked around. The boys were still dancing and no one else around her seemed to notice what had just happened. She didn't see anyone who looked like they did it. No one was saying, "Excuse me," or "I'm so sorry, are you okay?" A few seconds ago the music was fantastic, now Vita had a splitting headache. She didn't want to bail on her friends so she stayed but was very thankful when everyone was ready to leave an hour later.

When she got home at one-thirty that morning, she took two extra-strength Tylenol, hopped in the shower, drank a big glass of water and slipped into bed. At least tomorrow was Saturday and she could sleep in.

At seven o'clock in the morning Vita woke to pounding on her front door. "What the fuck," she groaned. Her head was still throbbing from the sucker punch from last night.

"Coming. I'm coming." She put on a silky robe, looked through the peephole to see who it was and opened the door. The security guard for the building was standing in her doorway.

"Good morning Miss Vita. I'm sorry to wake you so early but your car has been broken into." Vita stared blankly at the man. *Did he just say my car was broken into?* She continued the blank stare as he repeated himself.

"Was anything stolen?" she asked.

"I'm not sure ma'am but if you could come downstairs."

"Yes, yes, of course. Let me put some clothes on. Give me a minute." Vita closed the door and quickly put on a pair of sweats, a t-shirt and flip flops then followed the security guard down to the parking garage. Her assigned parking spot was on the third floor and as they approached the car she could see shattered glass on the ground. The passenger side window was smashed. Vita looked inside and nothing appeared to be missing.

"It appears to have happened just a few minutes ago," the security guard told Vita. "A resident on their way to their car heard glass breaking and yelled out which must have scared away the burglar," the security guard said. "Otherwise it could have been much worse."

Rattled, Vita thanked the man and headed back upstairs. "You should file a police report," the security guard called after her. "Just in case something was stolen that you can't see right now." Vita stopped, turned around and gave the security guard a weak smile and a thumbs up.

Vita couldn't believe her rotten luck the last couple of weeks. First she had razor blades in her tires, then she got hit on the head on the dance floor, then her car was broken into. *Am I just going through a rough patch or is this karma coming back on me for something?* She started thinking back on the last few months of her life, what she'd done, friends she'd hung out with, co-workers ... anyone whom she may have wronged. And then it hit her, "Kristen!"

She hadn't seen Kristen since that morning at the coffee shop. "No," she said out loud. "No way!"

Since Vita was already up with no chance of going back to sleep, she decided to get the car situation taken care of early. She called her local police station and reported the break-in. She was told she could pick up a copy of the police report Monday after two and that it would cost her fifty cents for a copy. "Seriously?" Vita moaned into the phone. "I'm the one violated here and you're charging me to get a copy of my police report? Unbelievable," she said to no one ... the person on the other end had already hung up. Next she called Blue, the apartment complex handyman, and asked if he could put plastic on her window until she could get it fixed. Lastly she called around to glass repair shops and got a few estimates on the cost of repair. She scheduled an appointment with a mobile repair shop who could fix it Monday morning.

To try and calm down Vita started cleaning her apartment. She vacuumed, dusted, mopped the hardwood floors, cleaned the bathrooms, changed her linen, watered all the plants and then went grocery shopping for the upcoming week. First stop: Trader Joe's to pick up multiple bottles of wine. She bought six bottles of her favorites; a California Zinfandel, Pinot Noir and Syrah. She picked up three bouquets of fresh flowers to boost her spirits, flowers always made her feel better no matter what she was going through. Next she went to her local Farmer's Market for fresh fish, fruits and veggies. She was going to have a great night. She texted her neighbor to see if he had plans for the night and to invite him over for dinner if he didn't.

Vita decided not to tell anyone except the police what was happening to her. After filing the police report, she received a follow-up call from one of the officers from the precinct. He told her to be careful and aware of her surroundings and to call him if anything else suspicious happened.

Across town Kristen was packing her last box. She had gotten a promotion and was moving to Los Angeles. She was excited about getting a new start and leaving the nonsense with Vita behind her. She almost got caught when she slipped past the security gate of Vita's apartment and broke the car window! That was enough. *I'll see her again one day. This is definitely not over. I'll eventually get my revenge for her making me fall for her and then tossing me aside. But time to put it away for now.* Kristen tipped the movers and thanked them. She then handed her keys to her landlord and thanked him too. She gave her apartment the once over, grabbed her bag and the last box of personal items and shut the door on her plot against Vita and the city of Chicago.

After a few tense months with no other odd occurrences, Vita felt safe. Months turned into years and she chalked it all up to a string of rotten luck. She never told anyone about what happened or who she thought was responsible. She heard that Kristen had moved to California and felt a huge sense of relief. If Kristen was responsible for flattening her tires and breaking her window, good riddance! It had to be her since all the vandalism stopped once that nut moved out of state. "Crazy bitch," Vita said out loud.

PRESENT DAY

When Vita's cell phone rang, she jumped. It was her friend and upstairs neighbor, Dillon. "Are you looking at the news? Did you see that sexy superhero pick up that car and save those people?" Vita was silent. "I don't think I've ever seen anything so hot," he exclaimed in obvious excitement. "V, you there?"

"Yeah, I'm here. I'm watching the news now and yes she's a bad ass."

"She looks a lot like you, don't you think V? She's your height and the two of you have the same hair."

"No we don't," Vita yelled trying to quickly get him off that topic. Vita's phone kept buzzing as they finished talking. She looked and had text messages from friends talking about the woman in the news. A few of them mentioned that the hero bore a striking resemblance to Vita. She texted them all back with generic talk about the superwoman but made no mention of their similarities.

The story was on the news for weeks, online sites ran wild with it and a Facebook page was created called Friends of the Sexy Superhero which had two hundred thousand likes after only five days. A very talented graphic artist even drew out the scene of the accident and rescue and posted it which drew even more likes. Scores of videos were posted on YouTube and Instagram of the rescue and flight.

Vita started wearing her hair in a ponytail and dressed in flats and sunglasses to try to stop all the looks she was getting and strangers stopping her asking if she was the superhero. But looking like the superhero everyone was fixated on did have its privileges. At bars strangers bought her drinks and people let her go ahead of them in grocery stores. At restaurants, owners and managers asked if her meal was satisfactory and most nights they comped it. Even cab drivers let her ride for free. And they all thanked her for what she did. It didn't matter that she denied being the woman in the news, no one seemed to care; they wanted to show appreciation on the off chance she really was the mystery woman.

One morning while waiting in line at a local coffee shop, Vita felt someone staring at her. She turned to her right and saw a beautiful woman smiling at her. Shyly Vita smiled back.

"May I help you?" The clerk behind the counter asked.

"I'll have a skinny café mocha please," Vita answered. She pulled out her wallet but the clerk said her order had already been paid for.

"Skinny café mocha," another clerk yelled from behind the pickup counter.

"That's me. Thanks," Vita said. She noticed the woman that had been smiling at her sitting at a table in the corner.

"Excuse me," Vita said as she stood in front of the smiling woman. "Thanks for the coffee."

Keeping the warm expression, the woman said, "How do you know it was me who bought it?"

"You were smiling at me the hardest so I just assumed. Am I wrong?" Vita asked.

With a sly grin, the woman said, "No, you're correct. It was me. It's the least I could do for the woman who saved the lives of those three people the other day."

Vita just stared at her. "I'm flattered but that wasn't me!" After a few uncomfortable seconds Vita said, "Well, I've got to get to work but again, thanks for the coffee." The two women locked eyes for two long seconds and then Vita turned and left.

When Vita was gone the woman reached into her bag, picked up her cell phone and turned off a voice recorder.

At the Four Seasons Hotel on Fourteenth Avenue in Atlanta, Toni paid the tab at the bar and made her way upstairs to a suite on the forty-first floor. She had barely gotten one foot in the door when she heard, "Did you get it?" It was early evening and the sun was beginning to set. Kristen was on the balcony enjoying the beautiful Atlanta skyline; a glass of champagne in one hand and a cell phone in the other. "I told you to text me after you got her voice recorded."

Toni took a seat on the balcony. "I know but I listened to the recording a few times first to make sure I got all our conversation and then I guess I forgot to text you."

"*Um hum*," Kristen mumbled deep in thought.

Vita couldn't concentrate on the report she was working on. It was due in an hour and she had barely even started it. Her hands were on the keyboard and an empty spreadsheet was staring her in the face but her mind kept wandering back to the woman at the coffee shop. She was a beautiful color, one that didn't quite tell you what race or nationality she was. She was a beautiful tan, like so many people Vita saw around Atlanta. She appeared to be about five feet nine inches tall, and had great hair. Her hairstyle was in a Mohawk cut, straight all over except for the top which was coiffed in the most perfect swooping style. It reminded Vita of another woman she had seen at the door of The Basement in East Atlanta, also great hair. Vita caught herself daydreaming of running her fingers through the hair of the stranger who paid for her coffee.

Suddenly her cell phone rang and snapped her out of it. It was her boss asking how the report was coming.

"Almost done. I'll have it to you in the next half hour."

Later that night, Vita and a few friends met for drinks after work at Apres Diem. The restaurant had a great lounge, nice vibe and a great patio which was perfect for people-watching and the drinks were amazing! The friends settled on a sofa that was partially outdoors with a great view of the crowd.

Vita walked to the bar to get a drink and met Tiffanie; they introduced themselves while waiting for their drinks. Tiffanie was twirling her hair and Vita was stretching her legs.

It had been a week since Vita had saved those people and she could tell by the way Tiffanie was looking at her that she thought this woman at the bar was the superhero. "I'm not her," Vita said without Tiffanie saying one word.

"I didn't say anything," Tiffanie laughed.

"I know you didn't but I could tell by the way you're looking at me that you think I'm the superhero everyone's talking about."

"Okay," Tiffanie said shaking her head realizing it was a sore subject and dropping it. They started talking a little and exchanged numbers after about fifteen minutes, each needing to leave to get back to their friends. "Call me tonight," Tiffanie called as she walked away.

Vita got home around two-thirty in the morning, took a shower and then picked up the phone to call Tiffanie. She hesitated for a minute thinking it may be too late but she called anyway. Tiffanie picked up on the second ring. They began talking and the conversation just flowed. They spoke about their past, where they were raised, their parents, where they went to school, relationships and a whole lot more. Vita noticed there weren't any gaps or pauses in the conversation. Three hours later, they hung up. Tiffanie had tried to talk about the superhero again but Vita shut her down. She made it clear that she wasn't that woman and didn't want to talk about it anymore. Tiffanie agreed but silently said to herself, *For now!*

At ten-thirty the next morning Vita was awakened by a thumping sound coming from the apartment upstairs. Neighbor Dillon was up early preparing for a party he was deejaying that night. She sent him a text asking if he wanted to come down for coffee in a few.

Hell yeah, he texted back. **See you in 15.**

Vita had been in her apartment for a little over a year. She lived on the Northwest side of Atlanta between Howell Mill Road and Northside Drive near one of her favorite restaurants: Yeah Burger. She loved the area which had a combination of apartments, condos, townhouses, restaurants, shops, bars, parks and businesses. She and Dillon met in the elevator of their building and became immediate friends. He was a cool, handsome young guy who listened to hip hop and rap and was a great cook. He was a pescatarian who ate fish, fruit, vegetables and grains. Dillon's number one passion was music and he worked for himself creating beats, doing social media updates for small businesses, recording educational raps for school kids, cooking meals for private parties and events and deejaying.

But Dillon's dream was to perform and distribute his own music. He had at least three ongoing music projects that Vita knew about; he was always busy, always coming and going. It was rare that he was up before noon so the job tonight must be a big one. A special gift he had was to know when Vita was hungry. He would text her and bring her a taste of one of his latest culinary creations. He brought her dishes like sautéed kale over quinoa with seared tuna, eggplant parmesan sandwiches on toasted ciabatta bread, lentils and potato and leek soup. He could whip up a sauce in minutes and was always topping things with homemade vinaigrettes, pesto and something disgusting sounding called nut cheese—nuts and olive oil pureed into a spread—which was surprisingly good. Anything he brought, Vita ate. She ate chicken and on very rare occasions lean red meat but she could easily become a pescatarian with this flow of good food coming at her.

Vita hadn't seen or spoken to Dillon since the whole superhero thing. He had been in New York City for a music conference the last four days and although he had tried calling and texting Vita, she hadn't responded. She didn't really want to answer his questions or try to explain the similarities between her and the woman who saved those people but today she did consider confessing, telling him the truth that it was her so there was someone to talk to about this. But then she thought the time wasn't right and who knew what the consequences would be?

Thirty minutes later, Vita heard a knock at the door. She had washed up, put her hair up and put on her comfy sweat suit and slippers. It was a beautiful summer morning so she opened her patio doors. She and Dillon could sit on the small patio and catch up. "Dillon," Vita said smiling ear to ear when she opened her door and saw him. "I've missed you!"

"What up V," Dillon exclaimed, pulling Vita close and giving her a big hug.

"Come on, let's sit outside."

Dillon handed Vita a carafe of freshly brewed Columbian coffee and followed her to the patio. "So what's going on Dillon? How was New York? I know you've been trying to reach me but things have been crazy for me the last few days so I'm sorry for not getting back to you."

Dillon didn't say a word. He just stared at her. "What? Are you trying to pretend you don't know what I wanted? You know what I called for! What the fuck V! You know what," Dillon said as he jumped to his feet.

"What?" Vita knew what was coming.

"You look exactly like the woman superhero that's all over the news who saved those people after that car accident. That's what. I know it's you! You're the bad ass that lifted the car off that dude and saved him from being crushed!" Vita said nothing. "Tell me the truth V. It's you isn't it? It's gotta be you. She looks just like you, same height, same slammin' body, same hair." He was still standing up firing questions at her a mile a minute. "Corey's asking me if it's you. Shelby thinks it's you! We all know it's you!" He finally took a breath and put his hands on his hips.

"I need a shot. Got any Tito's?" Dillon asked walking to the kitchen.

"Yeah, in the freezer."

Finding the cold vodka, Dillon poured two full shots. He started towards the patio then turned around and grabbed the bottle with the heel of one hand while balancing the shots, one in each hand. He thought that maybe if he got Vita a little tipsy that she'd confess and tell him the truth. "Here's to the truth," Dillon shouted, raising his shot glass to Vita. They did two more shots before drinking their morning coffee.

"Do you know how stupid you sound thinking I'm a superhero? First of all, people don't fly." Dillon looked at Vita as she spoke. "Who do you think I am, Superman or something? Personally I think the whole thing is a hoax. Somebody tampered with the news footage or something." Vita knew she wasn't convincing him one bit but she wanted to get off this subject and tell him about Tiffanie and the girl from the coffee shop.

Just when she thought they were off it, Dillon jumped up and said, "Then how do you explain all the videos people took on their phones and posted on Facebook and Instagram?"

Frustrated, Vita snapped back, "I don't know Dillon. I can't explain it. All I can tell you is that it's not me! I'm not her!" Vita stood up. "Thanks for the coffee but I've got to clean this dirty apartment. Let's have dinner soon. I'll call you." Vita hugged Dillon and hurried him out. She was tired of the questions and wanted to relax a little before heading out to meet Tiffanie. Tiffanie wanted to come over but they had just met last night and as much as Vita liked her, that was a little too quick to have her over. She seemed normal but these days one could never be too careful. And besides, Vita wasn't ready to get serious with anyone. Well, anyone except that woman from the coffee shop.

Vita plugged her iPad into a portable speaker system, turned on her favorite radio station and started cleaning up. She cleaned for hours stopping a few times to snack, take a few calls, play a few hands of Scrabble on her iPhone and grab a few minutes here and there of Law & Order. It was getting late and she was putting away some dishes from the drainer when she heard beeps from the emergency broadcast system. She began to feel that burning again on her stomach. The emergency broadcast said two children ages two and four years old were abducted in a carjacking in Hampton, GA, about thirty miles from Atlanta and were last seen heading south on I-75.

After the broadcast, Vita lifted her shirt and there it was, the ankh as big as day covering her entire stomach. Her body started tingling. "Oh no. It's happening again!" Vita ran upstairs to the roof and she barely made it when all of a sudden, another

BOOM! CRACK!

But this time Vita wasn't knocked unconscious. She watched the entire thing happen. First, a new outfit seemed to grow from her feet to her neck. It slithered slowly up her body like a second skin. Magically her feet were covered with the same boots, the ones with the high heels that were amazingly comfortable the first time the transformation happened. The outfit was a nice purple color, not too gaudy for a superhero outfit, topped by a black lycra and purple top with a belt that fit snuggly around her waist. And she even had nice gloves that completed the outfit. Her hair had also grown about 4 inches and it felt thicker than it had just a few minutes ago.

Dressed in this new outfit, Vita walked to the edge of the roof and looked down. *So how do I take off and fly?* She didn't remember much from before. She didn't really remember the transformation at all from the last time, the outfit covering her clothes, especially not her hair growing longer. Besides, it was only when she felt that her life was in danger that she just flew. She hadn't thought about it, it just happened. But this time was very different.

She didn't want to jump off the side of the building and go splat all over the sidewalk. She decided to take a few practice jumps. She walked to the other side of the roof, ran a few steps and sort of hopped. To her surprise she was airborne and landed all the way on the other side. *Humph*, she thought. *Not bad!* Vita looked into the night sky and to her amazement could see in the far distance the missing van that was reported on the radio and the missing children. The license plates matched and the description of the children and their abductor matched. The kids didn't appear to be in any danger and Vita thought that's why her superhero transformation and powers didn't come on as fast or extreme as before. *Maybe the worse the crime, accident or eminent danger, the quicker the change!*

"Time to save the children," she whispered to herself. And with that, she jumped off the side of the building and again was airborne.

Vita flew above the tall Atlanta buildings, weaving her way along until she was directly behind the van. She lifted the van a few feet above the ground so the children wouldn't be too scared and guided it into the parking lot of the Hampton Police Department. She quickly flattened the tires using a sharp knife-like object that appeared out of nowhere on the right cuff of her outfit. *I wonder what other secret gadgets and compartments this suit has.*

The van was quickly surrounded by Hampton police officers. The children were safely taken to a secure location and the driver, the children's

father, was arrested. Vita knew that
security footage of the parking lot would
show the flying van being placed in the
parking lot but she was sure to land the
van near a line of parked cars where she
could crawl behind one of them and not
be seen when she placed the van down
and flattened the tires. They may have
seen the van flying but they didn't get a
clear view of a face on the superhero
body. She had learned her lesson. She
flew home this time without all the
hassle of a crowd with cameras.

The next day was a Sunday. Vita
and Tiffanie agreed to meet for brunch
at Le Petite Marche in Kirkwood at one.
The weather was lovely; low humidity,
bright sunlight and a perfect day to be
outside. Arriving first, Vita chose a table
outside. Tiffanie was late so Vita ordered
a Bloody Mary and sat back to wait. She
liked hanging out in Kirkwood. It was
one of those hidden gems located within
the city of Atlanta and close to other
historic neighborhoods like East Lake,
Candler Park, Oakhurst and Edgewood.
Kirkwood was one of those
neighborhoods that you read about or
hear about on the news where the poor
and elderly were being pushed out by
yuppies moving back into the city and
buying dilapidated tear downs or vacant
lots to build new homes and remodeling

older homes and turning them into beautiful showplaces.

As Vita sat waiting she watched people riding their bikes up the hill on Hosea Williams Drive; a mother jogging with dogs, other mothers with carriages and others walking casually to coffee shops, bakeries and other shops and restaurants in the area. Kirkwood gentrification: the process of renewal and rebuilding accompanying the influx of middle class or affluent people into deteriorating areas that often displaced poorer residents. Despite the label, Vita would have loved to live there. The average price for a new home was two hundred seventy-nine thousand dollars or higher so it wasn't within her reach now but she could dream.

Tiffanie finally showed up thirty minutes late. She apologized profusely saying she got a late start, had to stop for gas and then got lost. Vita didn't mind at all and told her so. Tiffanie was a nice looking woman, in her mid-thirties, a nurse who graduated from Emory University and was pursuing a career as an anesthesiologist.

She really talks a lot, Vita thought. Two hours later Vita was ready to go.

As they were leaving Tiffanie said, "Hey, a friend is having a few people over tonight for a pool party, you know, a get together for a few friends. She's got a beautiful house off of Northside Drive in the city. She's a little older, in her late forties I think, and an attorney. From what I've heard, she always has great parties."

"Can I let you know a little later?" It was a Sunday and Vita had a busy day at work tomorrow and wasn't sure she was up for a late night Sunday party. Also, she wasn't sure she wanted to spend any more time with Tiffanie. She was nice to look at but was a little self-absorbed for Vita's taste. At brunch the lovely but chatty Tiff mostly talked about herself, her job, her boyfriend; although Vita could have sworn she was coming on to her. She asked very few questions of Vita and whenever Vita did speak, all Tiffanie would say was, *Mmmm*, like she wasn't really listening or didn't care what Vita was saying because she was so eager to talk more about herself. It was annoying.

But on the other hand, Vita was intrigued at the possibility of meeting some interesting, intelligent people. And she loved the sprawling homes on Northside Drive. Along with Kirkwood, Northside Drive was another area where she might want to live one day.

Vita texted Tiffanie at five-fifteen saying she was up for the barbeque and asking for the address. She thought it

was best to take her own car for two
reasons; one she didn't want Tiffanie
offering to pick her up because then
she'd know where she lived and two she
might want to leave earlier or later than
Tiffanie. *Taking your own car is always
the best move,* Vita thought to herself.
*And who knows. I might meet someone
I'm really interested in.*

Vita dashed off to the nail salon
to get a quick mani/ped and an eyebrow
and lip wax. Then other small
preparations. There was nothing to do
about her vehicle. Her car was older but
always washed once a week, it was ready
to go so as to not make a bad impression
on new people. It wouldn't impress, but
since she took pride in keeping it up; it
would just kind of be invisible. It was all
paid off and she was going to get every
mile out of it she could, at least until she
got a good promotion at work.

Vita got home from the nail salon
in plenty of time to enjoy a hot shower
and a glass of wine. She turned on music
and danced around as she got dressed.
She decided to wear blue striped DKNY
cutoff jeans she scored at Marshall's at a
great price, a white cotton tank and
orange leather flip flops. Tiffanie
mentioned it was an outside party so to
dress casual. With long hair up in a
ponytail, light makeup, dangling
earrings, lip gloss, Raffia tote with

leather trim—she headed out in high spirits.

They agreed to meet at Publix on Peachtree Street in Buckhead at eight. The sun was just going down and it was a beautiful spring night, a great night for a party. Tiffanie led in her car with Vita following closely behind. Tiffanie turned onto West Paces Ferry Road, an expensive street where the governor's mansion was located, then turned right onto Northside Drive. A few turns later and they were there. From the looks of the cars lining the street in front of the house, it seemed to be a nice turnout. The two had to walk a little ways to get to the house and then more walking up the long driveway. Both could hear music coming from the backyard so they headed that way.

Vita almost stopped in her tracks when she got to the backyard. It was so beautiful, like something out of a magazine or on one of those real estate reality shows featuring the rich and famous. The grounds were professionally landscaped with a pool, outdoor living area, bar, fireplace, love seats and couches that looked like they'd suck you in and never let you go if you sat in them. Tiffanie saw someone she knew and left Vita to go say hi so Vita made her way to the bar and ordered a margarita. As she stood there, she noticed a few women pointing at her and whispering to their friends. Obviously they were thinking what everyone thought when they saw her, that she was the superhero woman. Thankfully it didn't last that long so Vita was able to forget about it and enjoy the party. She watched as the female bartender filled a shaker with ice, added a generous pour of Jose Cuervo Especial Silver, fresh lime, a splash of orange juice and gave it a few shakes.

"Salt or no salt?" the cute little bartender asked.

"No salt," Vita replied. She took the drink from the bartender and started walking around. She didn't recognize anyone but smiled and said 'hi' to everyone she passed. She settled into a spot near the fireplace, a prime spot for people-watching. They'd been there for almost ninety minutes and Vita was having fun. She had joined in on a conversation about dating and how hard it was to find a good person, man or woman. Some women spoke about their online dating nightmares and one woman gave her online dating analogy, "Online dating is like shopping at the Goodwill. You have to sift through a ton of junk to find a gem." The stories were funny and made Vita glad she had never gone that route.

"Save my seat, will you?" Vita asked the woman sitting next to her. "Bar run. Anybody need anything from the bar?" Vita asked the group she was sitting with but there were no takers.

She had just sat down from her second trip to the bar and was sipping on another delicious margarita when she saw *her*: the woman from the coffee house. She was wearing a beautiful, sleeveless, orange dress and brown and macramé leather wedges. She looked taller than Vita remembered, with her high heeled wedges on. She was standing with a group of women exchanging pleasantries, slight kisses on the cheek and handshaking. Vita couldn't tell if she was alone or with someone. As she stared, she wondered what the woman's name was, how long she'd lived in Atlanta; all the things you want to know when you first meet someone you are interested in with that added question of if she was attracted to women.

Suddenly the woman turned, looked straight at Vita and smiled. Vita felt her stomach flip flop when she met the woman's gaze. *Oh my God, she's coming over here.* The woman was making her way over to where Vita sat and Vita felt her body temperature rising. Vita stood up to meet her.

"Hi," the woman said.

Vita began to speak but her mouth was so dry from being nervous, that nothing came out. All the saliva in her mouth had disappeared and she couldn't speak. She quickly took a swig of her margarita and finally said, "Hi yourself."

They stared at each other for what seemed like a lifetime to Vita before they spoke another word. Finally Vita said, "Nice seeing you again! I was wondering when I was going to see you again since I didn't get a name or anything the day you bought me that coffee."

The woman gave Vita a little smile and then said, "You would have gotten all that and more if you had stayed a little longer. You left in a hurry, remember?"

The woman had her cell phone in her purse and for a minute thought about turning on the voice recorder but decided against it. *Kristen doesn't need to know about this chance meeting,* she thought to herself.

"Let's go over there and sit," the woman said to Vita while grabbing a soft caramel colored hand. The woman only held Vita's hand for a few seconds but as soon as they touched, Vita felt goosebumps form on her arms.

"Let's get you a drink first," Vita said making a detour towards the bar.

"What's your pleasure?" Vita asked the smiling woman with no name.

"Margarita please."

They grabbed their drinks and sat near a tree that was surrounded by beautiful wildflowers, a small table and two Adirondack chairs. "First things first. What's your name?" Vita asked.

"It's Toni. Short for ShanTonica."

Vita laughed out loud. Toni laughed too. "What was your mom thinking?" They both laughed a little longer.

"Mine is Vita, so I guess my mom was not all that mainstream either." They spoke like old friends who had known each other for years, each interested in each other's stories, upbringing, friends, relationship statuses and anything else they could think of.

"There you are," Tiffanie called out as she approached Vita and Toni. "I've been looking for you. Hi, my name is Tiffanie," she said extending her hand to Toni. Tiffanie didn't wait for Toni to say anything before turning her attention back to Vita.

"You okay?" Vita asked Tiffanie.

"Yeah, I'm good. I was just wondering where you were. I haven't seen you for a few minutes but I see you're doing fine." Tiffanie spoke like she was mad and then stormed off.

"You need to take care of that?" a snickering Toni asked Vita.

"No and I'm not even sure what that was about." Vita explained how they briefly met then she and Toni talked for another hour or so before Vita decided she better go and find Tiffanie since they had come together—not as a date, but still as friends. Truth be told, she could have sat there and talked with Toni for the rest of the night.

"In case we don't meet up again tonight, take my number," Toni said. Vita took out her phone and gave it to Toni for her put the number in. "I'm calling me now so you'll have my number." After calling her own phone, Toni added her name to Vita's contacts and said, "Now we can stay in touch." Toni grabbed Vita by the hand and walked her over to a large tree a few feet away. She continued holding her hand, stroking it, moving her fingers in between Vita's. Vita stood with her back to the tree, Toni standing closely in front of her. They stood there looking at each other and then Toni moved even closer and kissed Vita slightly on her lips for a few seconds. *Her kiss is so soft,* Vita thought to herself as her mind spun in circles.

Although they were at a party, Vita heard nothing and saw no one but Toni. Toni kissed her again, this time with a little more force, a little tongue and for a little longer. Vita felt her nipples harden and her pussy getting wet. Toni took a step back and put her hand on Vita's heart. She smiled as she felt how fast Vita's heart was beating. They stood there looking at each other for a few more seconds and then Toni walked away. Vita watched and not knowing why, felt her heart sink a little. She shook her head in an attempt to get her head straight but she felt shaken up. This woman had definitely thrown her off her game. She was usually a lot cooler than this but since Toni asked for her number she must know exactly how Vita felt about her. Vita was embarrassed. She was never the one to wear her heart on her sleeve but here she was. "*Humph.* How is this going to go?" Vita said out loud to no one.

Vita found Tiffanie deep in conversation with a group of women and feeling no pain. They had been there for hours and it was time to go but Tiffanie was in no condition to drive. Vita said she'd give her a ride home and give her a ride back tomorrow to pick up her car if she couldn't get another ride. As they were leaving Vita scanned the party once more looking for Toni but didn't see her.

"Looking for your girlfriend?" Tiffanie slurred.

Vita ignored her and said, "Let's go."

When they got to the car, Vita got a text. It was from Toni. "Drive carefully beautiful. See you soon." *Toni must have seen me leaving.* Vita didn't know whether she should text back but she did. She texted back a smile emoji.

Toni made it home about two that morning. Kristen had called and texted her twenty times or more that night. *Crazy*, Toni thought. Walking up to her doorway, her phone rang again and again it was Kristen. "Stop calling me," Toni yelled out loud to no one, hoping she didn't wake her neighbors. Toni lived in an area of Atlanta called East Atlanta. She rented one side of a brick duplex on a quiet street not far from East Atlanta Village. Within walking distance of her house were restaurants, bars, clothing stores, a nice library and a branch of her local bank. Almost everything she needed was practically at her fingertips.

She was searching her bag for the house key but couldn't find it. For whatever reason, the house key wasn't on the key ring with all the other keys. "Shit, what the fuck did I do with my house key?" Then she remembered. She had taken her house key off the ring yesterday when she went running. The workout pants didn't have real pockets, just a little inside pocket big enough for one key. "Dammit! I forgot to put the key back on the key ring!" She always meant to hide a key outside but never got around to it. In a drunken frenzy Toni started shaking the doorknob on her front door, hoping somehow she could shake it open. All of a sudden the doorknob broke off in her hand. The entire doorknob and the screwed in doorplate around the doorknob all came loose. Luckily, she never locked the deadbolt when she left the house. Drunk and tired, she figured the knob was just loose so she picked up the outside doorknob, walked inside and stuck the doorknob back on both sides, closed the door, locked the deadbolt, threw everything on the floor, walked into her bedroom, took off her clothes and passed out.

Toni was awakened in the morning by a loud pounding on her front door. Feeling a hangover hit as soon as she opened her eyes, she stumbled to the front door. Kristen was standing on her front porch looking completely pissed. Toni opened the door and an angry Kristen stomped in.

"Where the fuck have you been? I've been calling you since yesterday! Why didn't you answer my calls or my text messages?" As she was talking, Kristen walked quickly through Toni's house, looking in each room to see if Toni had company.

"There's no one here," Toni said with an attitude.

"How do I know that?" Kristen snapped back.

"Because I'm telling you, that's why!"

Kristen ended her search in Toni's bedroom. She was still looking around and continued pressing Toni about her whereabouts yesterday.

"You want some coffee?" Toni asked Kristen as she made her way into the kitchen. *What did I do with my cell phone?* Toni thought. The last thing she needed was Kristen finding her phone and seeing the text message she sent to Vita.

Toni met Kristen a few months ago at a singles party a friend invited her to. They struck up a conversation, exchanged numbers, went on a few dates and slept together a few times. She liked the fact that Kristen lived in California because the woman could be a little clingy at times. She was in town enough on business for them to see each other regularly without it being too much. They never talked about being exclusive and the subject of dating other people never came up, but Kristen acted like they were a couple. And now this display of jealousy and distrust meant something might be coming to a head soon.

Initially Toni liked Kristen because she was a successful businesswoman who had her own shit. What she didn't like about Kristen was the possessive, controlling personality and the jealousy of everyone. It was like Kristen lived in fear of being rejected for someone else. The grilling about where Toni was, what time she got home, who she was with and who else she was seeing was getting worse with each visit. Toni wasn't hiding anything from Kristen but she didn't tell her everything either. She definitely didn't tell her about the party last night. When Kristen had asked Toni what she was doing Sunday night, Toni had told her she was going to dinner and to the movies with her friend Jonathan. Kristen didn't like Jonathan so Toni knew she wouldn't try and hone in on her night out.

Toni found her phone, put it on silent with screen lock and stuck it in the junk drawer in the kitchen. She made the coffee, poured two cups, added cream and sugar and headed back towards the bedroom. She couldn't even remember if Kristen said she wanted coffee but Toni knew why she was really there and what she did want.

"What happened to your doorknob?" Kristen asked. Kristen was naked and in Toni's bed by the time Toni got back to the bedroom. Toni sat on the side of the bed where Kristen was and handed her a cup of coffee.

Kristen started rubbing Toni's back. "Come back to bed," Kristen said in a sexy voice. Toni sighed slightly, removed her shorts and t-shirt and crawled into bed beside Kristen. "You know I've missed you," Kristen moaned in Toni's ear as she climbed on top of her. Kristen kissed Toni's neck, her nipples and her mouth. They kissed long and hard and by the time Kristen made her way down Toni's body, they were both ready. Kristen knew Toni liked oral sex more than anything and preferred it any day over being penetrated. She tolerated fingers and toys but nothing made her scream the way she did when getting her pussy eaten.

Kristen opened Toni's legs, lightly kissed the inside of both her thighs and then kissed her pussy. She kissed it like she kissed the lips on Toni' face, soft and with tongue. She parted her pussy lips and slowly slid her tongue up and down

Toni's clit. Kristen heard Toni moan softly and knew she had hit that spot. This time Kristen parted Toni's pussy lips with her right hand, using her index and forefinger to keep her pussy lips open and methodically licked her clit softly with her tongue. Kristen placed her left hand underneath Toni's left thigh and held her tight. Her body was moving to Toni's rhythm when she felt Toni's body stiffen, her moaning got louder and in a hushed voice she heard Toni say, "I'm coming!"

Kristen held her body tight, not removing her tongue but holding it in the exact spot that made Toni come. She pressed her tongue harder on that spot which only made Toni's body jerk uncontrollably. "No more Kristen, no more," Toni begged. Kristen kissed Toni's pussy one more time and then climbed on top of her. When she was sure she and Toni were clit-to-clit, she started grinding on her hard. Kristen came in less than two minutes. They both collapsed on the bed to rest.

"So what do you have planned for today?" Kristen asked Toni as she was putting on her clothes.

"I'm not sure but right now all I want to do is sleep," Toni answered.

The sex was good but it wasn't the reason Toni wanted to sleep more. She was truly tired and needed more sleep.

And she needed someone to come over and fix her doorknob. She still couldn't remember how that happened exactly.

"You know, we need to get back on that pet project of mine," Kristen said.

Growing tired of Kristen's company and under an overwhelming need for more sleep, Toni said with annoyance, "What's with you and that girl anyway? Why do you care if she's the superhero? So what if she is!?"

Standing, Kristen glared down at Toni and said, "You never told me what happened to your doorknob!"

Not this again. Walking towards the living room and hoping Kristen would follow; Toni walked up to the door and looked at the doorknob. She couldn't remember how the doorknob and the plate came off on both sides of the door. She kicked everything to the side as she heard Kristen coming.

"Let's get together and do dinner or something tonight," Kristen said to Toni as she walked towards the door.

"Sure. I'll call you later!" Toni gave Kristen a hug and opened the door with her fingers.

When Kristen was in her car and driving down the street, Toni closed her door and went back inside. She took a closer look at the doorknob. The screws

hadn't come loose like she thought; they
had broken off, snapped in half!

"What the! How could that have
happened?" Her mind started rambling.
"Do you know how strong you have to be
to snap screws in half?" She was
thinking out loud and then it hit her!
The kiss. It was the kiss. She *IS* the
superhero.

Vita woke up early Monday morning.
She relived her night, smiling every time
she thought about Toni. It was already
noon and she had texted her an hour ago
but so far Toni hadn't responded. Vita
must have checked her phone about
twenty times already but nothing.
Feeling completely disappointed, she
started straightening up. It was going to
be another beautiful day in Atlanta and
she didn't want to waste it. She had
hoped to have lunch with Toni today but
it didn't look like that was going to
happen. As she was thinking that, she
got a text. Hoping it was from Toni, she
rushed to the phone but when she
picked it up, the text was from Tiffanie

asking what she was doing for lunch and thanking her for driving her home last night. Vita felt a weird feeling in her stomach again, an ache of disappointment. She texted Tiffanie back saying she had errands to run at lunch but maybe they could get together later. Vita knew as she wrote the text that she was lying. She had no intention of seeing Tiffanie again so soon, one drunken night was enough for a while.

Vita had to get ready for work so after showering, getting dressed and checking her phone one last time—still no text from Toni—she left the house. A few hours later, finally the text she'd been waiting for all day came. It read: **Hi beautiful. Have dinner plans?** Vita read it and smiled from ear to ear. She wanted to play it cool and not respond immediately ... but who was she fooling? In less than one minute she texted Toni back saying she was free right after work. They texted back and forth for a few minutes and decided to meet at a quaint restaurant near Toni's house in East Atlanta that served excellent fish tacos, oysters and killer margaritas.

Vita got to the restaurant first, as was her usual habit, and picked a table on the patio. A few minutes later Toni arrived.

"Hi there beautiful," Toni said when she got to the table. Vita got up and gave her a big hug. She wanted to kiss her full on the lips but kept that desire pushed way, way down. They made small talk while looking at the menus and both ordered margaritas when the waitress came by to take their drink orders. They rehashed the party and the people they had met there, talked about the beautiful house, how nice it must be to have that kind of money and the parties they would have if they lived there. Vita started to ask Toni if she had a boyfriend, girlfriend or if she was in a relationship but secretly she didn't know if she really wanted to know just in case she didn't hear the answers she wanted. So she stayed away from that topic of conversation.

After they placed their orders, Toni said, "So are you gay or bisexual and are you in a relationship?" Vita was shocked by the abruptness of the questions. Toni obviously didn't have any of the inhibitions she had and she didn't beat around the bush either. She was direct and very matter of fact. Vita liked that about her, from the little she knew about her.

Suddenly Vita was distracted. "Oh no," Vita said softly. She began to feel that little twitch, the feeling she was getting accustomed to right before her

stomach started to burn. The feeling she
got letting her know disaster was
happening and someone needed her
help. "Not now," she whispered.

"What did you say," Toni asked,
smiling at Vita as she ate the last of her
fish tacos.

Vita stood up. "Be right back.
Bathroom break"

She went into the bathroom and
lifted up her shirt. She saw the imprint
of the ankh just below the surface of her
skin. After it had burned into her the
first time, it only became visible when it
itched and burned before a rescue. She
knew it was just a matter of time before
it would be fully visible on her bare skin
and she would be transformed into a
superhero. And it meant someone soon
was going to need her help. But how was
she going to break the news to Toni that
she had to leave? Vita got back to the
table and sat down.

"Everything okay?" Toni asked.

Vita looked at Toni and not
knowing what to say, she told her just
the simple the truth. "I have to leave."

Toni looked up, clearly
disappointed.

"Wait. Before you say anything,
let me explain," Vita softly said looking
directly into Toni's eyes. "Something's
come up and I can't go into detail right
now but I've got something really, really

important that I have to take care of.
And it can't wait. But, I want to continue
our date."

Toni looked at Vita and gave her a
little smile and said, "So this is a date?"

Vita smiled and stopped a
waitress that was passing by and asked
to borrow her pen. "Here's my address.
Meet me at my place later. I'll text you
when I'm on my way home and you can
meet me there. Can you do that? Can
you meet me later? I'm having a nice
time tonight and want to finish it. Will
you meet me later?" Vita asked again.

After a few tense moments of
silence, Toni nodded and said, "Yes, I'll
meet you."

Vita smiled. They both stood up.
"Here's my credit card. Just pay the bill
with this and give it back to me later,"
Vita said to Toni as they hugged. Vita
thought about how good Toni felt
wrapped in her arms. "I'll make this up
to you later tonight. I promise," Vita
whispered in Toni's ear. They looked at
each other and kissed on the lips.
Neither woman pulled away and the kiss
continued longer than either expected.
Feeling a sudden burning in her
stomach, Vita stepped back, looked at
Toni and left.

When Vita was sure she was out
of Toni's sight, she ducked into a dark
alley and held her breath as her body

started to transform. Although this was the third time, she wasn't used to it yet. She watched as a skintight suit covered her body, boots replaced her bare feet, her arms were wrapped in black snakeskin like gloves and then glasses covered her eyes to keep the bugs out as she flew through the night sky. Vita looked around one last time to make sure no one was watching, and seeing no one, she started running and then shot into the air, flying high into the night.

As soon as Vita was in the air, she saw the fire. She was flying northwest towards the Wells Fargo building in Atlantic Station, a mixed use community of retail and residential homes in Midtown Atlanta. As she got closer, the fire appeared to be coming from the W Hotel. Hovering in the sky nearby, she surveyed the situation.

The fire and police departments and even the local news channels were already on the scene working but there were still people trapped on the upper floors of the hotel. Vita saw people on balconies, other people without balconies trapped in their rooms with no way out and people on the street with their cell phones pointed upward, getting it all in to post on social media. Vita had to think quickly. There wasn't enough time to rescue each person one by one so she had to come up with a way to save them all *and fast.*

Nearby the build out of Cirque Du Soleil was under construction. Vita made her way inside the construction site on foot and within seconds dismantled three of the large tents that had been assembled. She tucked them and a few hooks under her arms and headed back towards the fire. As she got closer, she saw people pointing and clapping.

"It's her. The woman superhero! She's here to save us!"

Vita tied the tents to three balconies, flew down and began to secure them all to the ground with the hooks. Before she had even safely secured the first tent to the ground, the trapped people began sliding down. She quickly secured each tent, then flew back up to the balconies and pushed them all together so everyone could climb onto a balcony that had a tent attached. When everyone was sure they would be safe, they started jumping around and cheering. They started pointing up to the sky and hollering thank yous. Vita watched above and when she was sure everyone would be safe, she dashed out of sight.

She flew to the top of the Ikea building, sat on the roof and waited until everyone was safely on the ground.

When the last person was safe, Vita took off. She flew back to the alley to get the clothes she was wearing before the transformation. One thing she had learned was that if she could change out of the clothes she was wearing before the transformation, they wouldn't be ripped to shreds. She returned to the alley near the restaurant to get her clothes which she had tucked behind a dumpster, well hidden from plain sight. But when she reached behind the dumpster to retrieve them, they were gone! Obviously someone had seen her duck in the alley and had stolen her clothes, her shoes and her bag. At least she carried her phone and id with her. She had learned that lesson the first time she transformed too.

Feeling completely exhausted and exhilarated at the same time from this latest lifesaving adventure, Vita texted Toni to let her know she was on her way home and hoped she could still make it over. She had been gone longer than she thought and the no clothes situation didn't help. She had to walk the few miles to her apartment, taking the dark back roads so she wouldn't be seen in her superhero outfit. Finally Toni texted back saying she was on her way. Vita texted back for her to call when she was downstairs in case she was asleep. It was already after two in the morning and if everything went as planned, Vita knew she and Toni would be up all night. Vita showered and put on her best casual but sexy camisole and short set. She poured a glass of wine, opened the doors to the patio and laid on the couch looking outside to wait for Toni.

Toni was grabbing the last of her things for a night at Vita's when she heard a knock at the door. "You've got to be kidding me," she said out loud.

It was Kristen. Toni hated it when Kristen showed up out of the blue without calling. It was so rude! She quickly hid Vita's clothes, shoes and bag that she had taken from behind the dumpster. She wasn't sure what she was going to do with the goldmine she found but she knew somehow she was going to get paid for it by somebody.

She opened the door and let Kristen in. "What are you doing here so late?" Toni asked Kristen letting the annoyance show through. "You don't call first or anything? You can't just show up at my house anytime you want!"

"I've missed you," Kristen said, slurring her words. She was obviously drunk. Toni knew there was no way she was going to make it over to Vita's house tonight. She started to text her but decided against it because she didn't want to explain why she really couldn't come and she was too tired to come up with a good lie. She also knew that blowing her off would only make Vita want her more. For a moment Toni felt bad but didn't send another text. Curiosity trumped her annoyance with the drunken girl. Toni still wasn't sure of Kristen's motives. They didn't seem to be driven by money but something more personal but she hadn't shared the real reason yet. But she would in time, Toni was sure of it.

    Toni took a few deep breaths and led Kristen into the bedroom. She got her two aspirin and a big glass of water. Then she took Kristen's clothes off and put her to bed. Toni stared at the ceiling while listening to Kristen snoring loudly next to her. She couldn't sleep. She picked up her phone which was lying on the table next to her bed to see if Vita had called or texted, but she hadn't. As much as she tried not to admit it, she felt guilty. Her entire reason for meeting Vita the first time was for money. Kristen had promised to pay her one thousand dollars if she would help prove that Vita was the superhero. And she had already been paid five hundred dollars for the voice recording and figured the clothes and other personal items of Vita's were worth more than the agreed upon additional five hundred. And the worst part of all, she was starting to have feeling for Vita, real feelings.

She thought about Vita for the rest of the night until she drifted off to sleep next to Kristen.

At three-thirty in the morning, Vita's cell phone starting buzzing. "This girl is finally on her way," Vita said out loud. Smiling, she looked at her phone but it wasn't a text from Toni but Dillon. It said: **Heard your music on. You still up?** Before answering Dillon, Vita checked to see if she had any other text messages, particularly if she had nodded off and missed one from Toni. But she hadn't. Toni hadn't sent a text since the last one saying she was on her way. Vita texted Dillon back and said she was up. He texted back inviting her up to his apartment for shots, food and weed. It was exactly what she needed after saving lives and then getting stood up. "Fuck it," she said, grabbing her phone, keys, Tito's vodka and two shot glasses and headed upstairs.

When Vita got to Dillon's, she knocked but knew he couldn't hear so she walked on in. Dillon was out on his patio smoking.

"Hey there handsome," Vita yelled as she walked toward the patio.

"Hey sexy!" Dillon replied. He grabbed the Tito's and the two shot glasses and poured them a shot. Vita

knew she shouldn't mix wine and vodka
but *oh well.*

"Here's to saving lives," he said.
Both he and Vita downed their shots.
"Let's do another one," Dillon said
quickly. He poured two more shots and
they downed those just as fast. "Here V,
take a hit of this," Dillon said while
trying to give her a shotgun.

She stepped back. "No, I'm good
for now, gotta work in a few hours.
Maybe later."

"Ok, cool," Dillon said.

"Are you okay?" Vita asked.
"You're acting kind of weird."

Without hesitation, Dillon walked
inside and turned on the television. The
channel was on the local Atlanta station
and the news coverage was about the
fire and rescue at Atlantic Station. He
switched to another station and the
coverage was the same: "Superhero
strikes again, saves hundreds!!" Every
news station was covering it and he
showed her that it was the number one
trending topic on Twitter.

Vita turned off the television,
took Dillon's phone from him and put it
down, grabbed the vodka and poured
herself two more shots. She then
grabbed the joint he was smoking and
took three long hits.

"I love this song," Vita said as she
started dancing in the den. Dillon was

playing one of his old school mixes and Vita walked over to him and started dancing in front of him. They began dancing together in a drunken stupor, Vita turning around and grinding her ass into Dillon's crotch. He grabbed her around the waist a few times and slyly let his hand slip down to her ass. She twirled around, her head moving from side to side, her eyes closed as she let the music sweep her up and clear her mind. Every couple of seconds she thought of Toni but tried hard to push the thoughts away. *Stay in the here and now.*

Vita deliberately moved towards him, put both hands on his waist and placed her thighs inside his. They kept moving, doing a little more grinding than dancing. Dillon grabbed the Tito's and they did two more shots. Vita could see Dillon's eyes moving up and down her body. She wasn't wearing a bra and her hard nipples stuck out like pencil erasers under her camisole. She also knew that Dillon could see the crack of her ass as she danced in front of him. Suddenly Vita felt Dillon's hand untying the drawstring on her shorts. He was standing behind her and without warning his hands were inside her shorts, massaging her clit.

Vita didn't say no and didn't tell him to stop. She didn't look at him either. Her eyes were closed, her body moving to the rhythm of Dillon's fingers and the music. She was feeling no pain. It had been a long night so far and the lyrics of the Rolling Stones song ran through her head, "If you can't be with the one you love, love the one you're with!" Vita opened her eyes and kissed Dillon on the lips. That kiss led to a few more pecks on the lips and then a little tongue, all while he was still fingering her.

"Knock, knock!"

"Is that someone at your door at four-thirty in the morning?" Vita leaned back and looked at her host.

Dillon forgot he had texted another friend before Vita. The girl usually never responded so he hadn't given her a second thought. He gave Vita a chagrined look and nodded.

"Let her in," Vita said. "It's no big deal."

Dillon's friend Emily came in. They all did a few more shots, smoked a little more weed and then Vita left as the two of them started making out. It was now five-fifteen. Vita couldn't remember the last time she had been up so late; even saving lives hadn't kept her up this late. *That was weird*, she thought. *Me and Dillon! Who knows what would have happened if that girl didn't show up!*

She made her way downstairs to her apartment, turned her phone to silent, took a shower, put on her favorite pajamas and passed out.

"Toni wake up!" It was seven-thirty in the morning and Kristen was awake and dressed. Toni woke up, immediately feeling pissed. She held back from screaming at Kristen to get the fuck out of her house. Kristen shook her. "Are you awake?"

"Yes, I'm awake! What?"

"I just wanted to tell you that I'm leaving."

"Ok," Toni said. Inside she was screaming, *Then leave already!* Toni turned over and looked at Kristen. *How is she up so early after being so drunk?* Toni got up and walked Kristen to the door and unlocked it. Kristen stepped in front of her and starting explaining why she had to leave, what her plans were for later and some other things Toni had absolutely no interest in. Toni was looking at her but didn't hear the words, she just saw Kristen's lips moving. She envisioned pressing the palm of her hand up against Kristen's forehead and shoving her out the door.

"Are you listening to me?"

"What?"

"Are you listening to me?"

"Yeah, yeah, I'm listening, just waking up," Toni lied.

"Ok, then call me later!"

"I will," Toni lied again. Kristen gave her a scowl. "I promise, I will call you later," Toni said getting more annoyed by the minute. Suddenly Kristen moved forward and kissed her on the lips. Toni wasn't expecting the kiss so her lips were parted slightly. Kristen took that as more of an invitation than the hesitation which is what it really was. And the next kiss lasted longer and was a lot more intimate than Toni wanted it to be.

Vita woke up around nine-thirty to pee, checked her phone and saw one text from Toni, one from Dillon and two from Tiffanie. She didn't read any of them, she called in sick at work then put the phone down and climbed back into bed and slept for three more hours.

Vita awoke this time to a knock on her door. She got up, looked through the peephole and saw that it was Toni. *Shit.* She hadn't had a chance to wash her face, brush her teeth or run a washcloth over her ass! *Too late now.* Feeling a little nervous, she opened the door.

"Hi, I'm looking for a sexy, tall woman I had dinner with last night," Toni said. "We were supposed to meet up last night but unfortunately I wasn't able to make it and I'm here to apologize to her! Do you know where I can find her?"

"Come on in," Vita said smiling ear to ear. "I'm her roommate. Let me see if I can find her. If she's not available, is there a message I can pass on for you?"

"Yeah. You can tell her that I'm so sorry for not showing up last night and that something came up that I couldn't get out of and that I really wanted to spend some more time with her and to extend our great night together and to tell me what I can do to make it up to her."

Vita just stared at her. Heart racing. She wanted to kiss her right then and there but also wanted to tell her that she had hurt her feelings last night by not showing up or texting that she couldn't make it. But at the same time

84

she didn't want to seem clingy or controlling so early in the friendship. There was something else, too. A thought totally new to Vita. She didn't want to appear too vulnerable.

"What if I tell her what you said but she still doesn't want to see you?"

"*Humph*," Toni said. "Well, tell her that if she decides not to see me that this is what she'll be missing!" And with that Toni leaned in and kissed Vita full on the lips with a little tongue.

They kissed for a minute before Vita pulled back. "Come on in."

Sitting on the couch, Vita let down her guard. "Why didn't you text me back and let me know you weren't coming? I waited up all night for you," she lied.

Instead of answering, Toni kissed her again. "I'm sorry," Toni mumbled in between kisses. "It'll never happen again!" Toni got up from the couch, then kissed both of Vita's breasts slowly. Then Toni untied Vita's pajama pants, pushed them down under the curve of her butt and caressed one cheek of her ass, all while kissing her.

It was all moving so fast but Vita realized she didn't want to stop it. It was moving fast but somehow felt like it was all taking place in slow motion too, maybe because she wanted to remember it all, frame by frame. Toni stepped back and removed her own clothes. Taking the queue, Vita stepped out of her pajama bottoms.

"Turn around for me so I can see all of you," Toni said.

Without hesitation, Vita stepped back and slowly turned around; making sure Toni took in every inch of her. Pulling Vita to her, Toni mumbled hotly, "I wanna fuck you!"

Vita backed up a few steps until she was on the bed. Before she could even move to the head of the bed, Toni was on her. She was on top of her, kissing her and grinding on her pussy with a knee. Toni kissed Vita's breasts again, then moved down to her stomach and kissed it. She then kissed the tops of her thighs, then the insides of her thighs and then kissed her pussy. She kissed the top of it, the right and left sides and then the middle. And that's where she stayed.

Using both hands, she separated the warm soft lower lips and placed her tongue in the middle, directly on Vita's clit. Once she was positioned, Toni moved her left hand up Vita's body and grabbed her by the waist. Keeping her right hand in position, she kissed and slowly licked Vita's clit. After a few seconds, they were in rhythm, Toni moving to Vita's movements. Vita started moaning softly and although she

tried to control it, her moans grew
louder.

*Oh my god, it's happening too
fast!* She tried to slow her body down, to
think of something other than how good
Toni was making her feel but to no avail.
As much as she tried, she couldn't stop
it. Vita grabbed Toni's hair and squeezed
her legs closer, almost putting Toni's
head in a vice lock. Before she knew it,
she was softly moaning, "Yeah, right
there! Right there!"

Toni could tell Vita was about to
come but she didn't move. She kept
doing what she had been doing but
applying a little more pressure with her
tongue.

"Oh God," Vita moaned out loud.
"Oh God."

Toni didn't stop. She kept her
tongue in the exact spot that made Vita
come and kept applying the pressure.
Vita's body lifted up and down and Toni
moved with her, keeping her tongue in
place. When Vita stopped moving, Toni
laid still but didn't remove her tongue.
Finally, Vita lifted Toni's head and
looked at her, smiling.

"What do you want?"

"I want you," she said.

"I meant what do you want right
now? It's your turn."

"Oh," Toni smiled. "Turn over."

Vita turned over on her stomach and Toni got on top of her, grinding on her ass. At first Vita was moving with Toni's rhythm until Toni stopped her. Holding both of Vita's wrists down, Toni whispered, "Don't move! Just lay there!" Toni ground on Vita's ass and minutes later, she came. Vita rolled over and Toni collapsed on top of her, resting her head on Vita's stomach. Instinctively Vita began caressing Toni's head, running her fingers through her hair. They laid that way for a few minutes, neither one speaking.

"Have you fallen asleep on me?" Vita softly whispered. When she didn't get an answer, she knew Toni was asleep. She was snoring lightly and Vita didn't want to wake her but she had to pee. Vita began to touch Toni's ears, sort of tickling her trying to wake her up. After a few minutes, Toni woke up, looking embarrassed that she had fallen asleep. She moved to the side of the bed and when Vita came back from the bathroom, they stretched out there side by side.

A few hours later, Vita woke first and wondered when Toni was going to mention the latest superhero story. So far she hadn't mentioned it at their first dinner together at the restaurant near Toni's house and hadn't mentioned it in any of her text messages and hadn't mentioned it so far today. She was sure she knew it was her but maybe she didn't care about that. *Maybe she likes me for me, not for fame or fortune or anything. That would be really nice if that were true,* Vita daydreamed.

Toni got up and starting getting dressed. Vita didn't follow; she was lying on her side, still naked, watching Toni get dressed. "I've got some running around to do this afternoon but I'll call you later, okay?" Toni asked as she leaned over and gave Vita a quick kiss. "I had a nice time today. Maybe we could do this again real soon," Toni said grabbing the rest of her things.

"Definitely," Vita said with no hesitation. They walked to the door holding hands and kissed one more time before Toni left.

When Toni got to her car she called her friend Allison. "Hey Al," she said when Allison answered.

"Hi stranger. I haven't seen or heard from you since my birthday party six months ago," Allison said excitedly, glad to hear from her friend.

"I know. I'm sorry. I've been busy, running here and there and traveling," Toni responded. Allison was a talker so Toni had to get to the point quickly or she'd be on the phone for an hour without getting to the reason for her call. "Listen Allison, I'm about to run into the movie theater but need a favor."

"Sure, what do you need?"

Allison was a nurse at Piedmont Hospital and Toni knew she had been drawing blood since before she graduated nursing school. "I know this is going to sound strange but I need to utilize your nursing skills."

"Okay," Allison said sounding a little skeptical.

"It's not for anything criminal," Toni said sensing Allison's hesitation. "I need you to draw a few vials of blood for me. And I promise you it's mine and for my own personal use. And not for anything I need right now but just in case I do need it, I want to have it." Toni was done explaining and Allison was silent on the other end. "Listen Al," Toni pleaded. "I know it sounds crazy but can you do this for me please?"

Hearing the desperation in her voice, Allison quickly jumped in. "Sure girl, I can do it for you. Just leave my name out of it, whatever you're going to use it for. Okay?"

"Okay, I promise," Toni said.

Allison could almost hear Toni smiling. "When do you need to have it done?" Allison asked.

"How about now? I'm right around the corner from your house," Toni answered quickly.

"How did you know I was going to say yes?" Allison asked.

Toni didn't respond to that. Smiling she said, "I'll see you in a few minutes," and hung up the phone.

Allison and Toni met at a party years ago and although Allison was ten years older than Toni was, they became fast friends. Although Allison was married with a fantastic husband and two adorable kids, Toni knew she had a girl crush on her and today she used that knowledge to her full advantage. After exchanging pleasantries with Allison's husband and kids, Toni and Allison went to the bathroom where Allison drew two vials of Toni's blood.

"Thank you so much," Toni said when they were done. "You're a lifesaver!"

"No problem. Just remember to keep my name out of it," Allison said before handing over the vials.

"I promise." Toni made more small talk with the family and took the first opportunity she could to get out of that house. Toni wondered how much super power she had left after having her blood drawn. To test it she stopped at a Sports Authority, walked back to the free weight section and when no one was looking tried to pick up one of those machines muscle heads used to work their chest muscles. It had four hundred pounds on it: four fifty pound plates on each side, plus the bar. She looked around again to make sure no one was watching her, stood behind the machine and tried lifting it up by the seat, but she couldn't.

"*Hmph,*" she said after a little strain. She removed one hundred pounds and tried again but she still couldn't lift it. She removed two more plates, one hundred more pounds, and tried again. She was able to lift it a little, getting it off the floor but couldn't hold it for more than a few seconds.

She didn't try again but assumed she'd be able to lift the two hundred pounds, so left. On her way out a sales guy asked, "Can I help you with something?"

"Actually you can," Toni said. "Can you tell me how much that bench weighs with the weights and the bar?"

"Well you're looking at the four hundred fifty-five Olympic grip plates. With the accessory rack, dip bar and press attachment, you're looking at a weight capacity of approximately seventeen hundred pounds."

Rudely interrupting him, Toni said, "So without the weights and the bar, how much would you say it weighs?"

"Well it's pretty heavy and the bench is attached so you're probably

looking at about tree hundred and fifty
pounds or more. But like I said, the
weight capacity with the attachments is
a lot more if you want me to show you."

"No, that's okay but thank you,"
Toni said as she hurried out of the store.

At least she knew a little more
about the transference than she knew
before. It appeared that the powers were
transferred during any exchange of body
fluids like kissing or oral sex. And once
the sexual exchange happened, the
powers must have gotten into the
bloodstream. There was no other way to
explain how she could have picked up
that piece of gym equipment after
having sex with Vita only a few hours
ago. But she didn't know how long it
lasted after it was transferred and
exactly how powerful one could become.
And there was only one way to find out!

When Toni got home she dug
holes in two potatoes she had in the
refrigerator and put one vial in each
potato. She put the potatoes back in the
bag with the rest of the potatoes. No one
would ever look in there, she was sure of
it.

Unlike Vita, Toni didn't have to
get ready for work the next day. She
didn't have a traditional nine-to-five job
but still considered what she did work.
She had two men whom she saw
regularly who paid her rent, cell phone,

furnished her apartment, paid her utilities and paid her gym membership. They also gave her spending money to enjoy a social life. In exchange for the money, she provided sexual favors for the men, went with them on trips and even stayed with them at their homes when their wives were out of town. Many of her friends didn't approve but she didn't care. It was family legacy. Her mother got by doing the same thing, so why shouldn't she? It was what she knew and furthermore she was good at it. And she didn't have to get emotionally involved. To her, dealing with the two of them was a job, nothing else.

Toni took a shower and lay down on the couch to watch some television. Her phone rang again for the tenth time that day and it was from the same person: Kristen. Toni was all about making money and realized that she sold herself short by agreeing to the thousand dollars Kristen offered her to get proof that Vita was the superhero. She had all the proof she needed; the voice recordings, the clothes and the *pièce de résistance*, the blood she had drawn which she knew contained something so powerful that it could potentially make a person fly if they injected it—at least that was the hope. But the one thing she did know was that it would make anyone who injected it strong enough to lift a car and bend steel with their bare hands.

Toni wasn't sure how long the transferred powers would be in affect but she knew that with the two vials of blood in her fridge that she had captured lightning in a bottle. *How much would one vial be worth? Whatever it's worth, I'm definitely going to be selling it to the highest bidder!* She had to figure out how she would let it be known that she had it and convey the power it possessed to the people that might be willing to pay the most for this power. She would figure that out later but for now, she needed sleep. Her mind was tired and she had to keep pushing back those nagging thoughts her conscience was trying to bring to the forefront of her mind ... that what she was doing was wrong and that she really liked Vita, had real feelings for this lady and that this would hurt Vita so deeply there would be no chance of a long term relationship once this betrayal was found out.

After tossing and turning on the couch, Toni gave Kristen a call and told her she had an upset stomach and apologized for not returning the earlier calls. Then Toni called Vita, talked to her for a while, made plans to see her on Wednesday or Thursday, checked in with her two sugar daddies and then climbed into bed totally exhausted and trying to keep future plans straight. Her thoughts inexplicably went to her afternoon with Vita; how nice it was, how natural it felt and how easy it was to be around her. She drifted off to sleep with thoughts of Vita on her mind.

On the way home from Toni's, Kristen stopped by her favorite farmers market in Atlanta. It was only five minutes after eight in the morning and the parking lot was already full. She decided to park on the street even though it was going to cost fifty cents for the ten minutes in the market. She was in a hurry, so what the hell. After finding two quarters in her bag, Kristen put the first quarter in and turned the knob, put the second quarter in and turned but this time the knob didn't rotate.

"Dammit," Kristen yelled. She tried a few more times but still the knob wouldn't turn. Frustrated, she tried one more time and this time turned the knob with more force than before. Kristen heard something that sounded like a click. She looked at her right hand and the knob from the meter was in it! *What the fuck! What just happened?* Kristen thought, not wanting to move or speak out loud for fear she was still high and drunk from last night and possibly hallucinating.

"Last night *was* kind of fuzzy," she said to herself. "I could have been ruffied!" *But then how could I have driven to Toni's?* - - she thought some more. She quickly replayed last night in her head. She remembered driving to Toni's, knocking on the door, turning the new doorknob and trying to get in. And she remembered Toni giving her two aspirin and water. *So I was okay up to that point*, Kristen thought. *I guess this knob was loose.* Kristen had been in front of the meter for at least ten minutes and the time remaining still said ten minutes. She made a mental note of where she had parked for next time. "Great meter!" She mumbled.

Toni climbed back into bed and reached for her cell phone. She hesitated for a few minutes and then sent Vita a text message that said, "Sorry again about last night!" She waited and waited but Vita didn't text her back. Toni didn't know why she felt disappointed. She knew she and Vita would talk sometime that day but for some reason she couldn't shake a familiar feeling that was creeping up on her.

Meanwhile, Vita had a lazy rest of the day doing laundry, folding clothes, watching Law and Order and talking on the phone. She spoke to her parents whom she hadn't spoken with in over a week, reassuring her mother that she wasn't the superhero her friends were telling her looked like her daughter. She chatted with Tiffanie for a little while, promising to meet up with her Wednesday night to catch up and listen to some live music at BQE on Edgewood Avenue. It was a quiet day but she needed it, she was tired and needed a rest.

Later that afternoon Dillon gave her a call. "Hey V," he began. "Had a nice time with you last night. Too bad we were interrupted. Who knows where that was headed!"

"Yeah, it was fun," Vita said laughing a little. "How did the rest of your night go with your friend?" Vita asked Dillon.

"Actually, that's why I'm calling you. The weirdest thing happened when

you left. You saw that chick last night;
she wasn't hurting for a meal."

"Yeah I noticed," Vita said.

"Anyway," Dillon continued. "She
obviously wanted to fuck, so after you
left I lifted her fat ass like she weighed
twenty pounds! It was like I had super
human strength or something!" Vita was
silent. "She probably weighs thirty
pounds more than I do," Dillon went on.
"I don't know what it was but I was able
to lift her and carry her into my
bedroom. Then I held her up, her back
against the wall and fucked her standing
up," he said in the most excited voice
Vita had ever heard him use. "Do you
know how much strength it takes, how
strong I'd have to be to lift her and fuck
her at the same time?" Dillon was
asking; his questions were rhetorical.
"All I'm gonna say is that I think it was
that kiss you gave me that gave me the
extra strength!"

"What?!" Vita yelled. "What does
you fucking that big bitch have to do
with me?"

"Relax, relax," Dillon pleaded.
"I'm just saying. How else would you
explain it?"

"I have no idea what you're
talking about," Vita said, suddenly
needing to get off the phone, hoping
what he was saying was not true. If
somehow her powers were transferrable

through kissing, what kind of powers was Toni experiencing right now considering the sex they had!

"I'm not doubting what you're saying," Vita finally said to Dillon, "but let me process what you're saying, think about things."

"So, are you her?" Dillon asked quietly.

"Let me process what you're telling me and I'll give you a call later. And Dillon thanks for not running to the news outlets or posting this online."

"No problem V. You're my friend. I wouldn't do that to you!"

"Thanks Dillon. That's why we're friends." But Vita wasn't that naive. She figured Dillon was staying silent so far because he knew something would come of this and he would make and do more with her than going against her. And he was correct.

Vita didn't get much done for the rest of the day. If what Dillon was saying was true, was Toni aware of the powers that had been transferred to her? And if she was aware of it, why hadn't she said anything about it? Or maybe it was only transferrable through heterosexual relations! "That's absurd," Vita said out loud. She thought about how many times she had kissed Toni: at the party, at dinner and yesterday. If Dillon noticed and she only kissed him briefly, how much superhero powers did Toni experience? And how long did it last?

Suddenly the first red flag about Toni went off in Vita's head. She called Dillon back, pushing a feeling of panic down so she could think clearly.

"Hey V, what's up?"

"Question for you," she said. "Did you have any warning signs before you lifted the fat girl up? Did you feel something had changed with you? Did you feel any different?"

"No," he said. "If that girl hadn't come over, I don't think I would have realized it. Maybe if I had tried lifting something or doing something that required me to use a lot of strength, maybe I would have noticed. Hard to say."

"Okay," Vita said. "Still trying to wrap my head around it. I'll give you a call tomorrow, okay?"

"Okay," Dillon said. "Talk to you then V."

The next morning Vita gathered her things and headed off to work. She got off the elevator, walked through the lobby and as soon as she stepped out onto the sidewalk she was mobbed by news reporters and paparazzi. They were snapping pictures of her faster than she could blink, blocking her way so she couldn't move and asking her questions so fast she couldn't get her bearings. Luckily she had put on her sunglasses while on the elevator so at least she was shielded a little. Finally, she was able to push through a small opening in the crowd and ran all the way to the Marta station.

When Vita got to work it was the same thing; co-workers taking her picture as she walked down the hallway, staring at her and pointing as she walked by, whispering to their friends and texting on their phones. *What is going on? What brought me to the media's attention?* - - she wondered.

She walked to her cube and there it was on the front page of the AJC, her picture side by side with a picture of the superhero! *Where did they get that picture of me?* It looked to be in a social setting so she was sure the picture had come from a friend. But you couldn't deny the resemblance: same face, same height, hair length and build. The headline read: **Sexy Superhero Saves City!** Underneath the two pictures were smaller pictures of the Atlantic Station rescue and her first rescue of the people trapped underneath the car.

Her work phone rang; the boss asked if she could come to her office. "Be right there," Vita said. *This can't be good.* Vita sat in her boss' office and listened while the boss tried explaining why they were letting her go. She explained that management thought this issue had become a distraction and thought the publicity would reflect negatively on the company. She said they would write Vita a glowing letter of recommendation for her next employer and would give her two week's severance pay, her two week's unused vacation pay and three unused sick days. So, all-in-all over four week's pay. Vita asked if she could speak with someone in accounting so she could claim exempt on her W4 so no taxes would be withheld. Her boss agreed and Vita filled out the necessary paperwork. At least she would get a few more hundred dollars in her last paycheck. She was sure they'd lump it all into one check so at least she'd be safe for a few months. After packing her box and saying goodbye to a few co-workers, she left the building in total shock. *At least I'm a superhero and can rob a bank if things get desperate.* But in her heart she knew she could never do that. She just wasn't that kind of person.

Vita took the train home thankful that it wasn't rush hour. She couldn't imagine the humiliation she would have felt taking a packed train home with her box of personal belongings and everyone staring at her, knowing she was a superhero *and* fired. And the ironic thing was, she was actually helping people and saving lives. But where did that get her? Fired! Vita went in the back door of her building to avoid the few photographers that were still camped out.

Once she got home her thoughts turned to how she was going to pay rent, the cell phone bill and all the utilities and other little things. She didn't want to call her parents which would open up another can of worms. She'd have to explain what happened, why she got fired, what she'd been doing and all that. Luckily, the story she'd given them about not being the woman superhero had stuck and they hadn't brought the subject up in a while but if she called for money, who knows where that conversation would lead. So Vita didn't call. All she knew was that she had a month to figure something out.

Vita had put her phone on silent when she was with her boss and had forgotten to turn the volume back up. When she looked at her phone, she had twenty missed calls and thirty or more text messages. Obviously all of her friends had seen the paper and she assumed all the calls were from reporters. She needed to get out of there, to go somewhere where she could think. She scanned through her calls and thankfully there was one from Toni. Vita called her back and Toni answered on the first ring.

"Hey, are you okay?" Toni asked before Vita could say a word.

"Yeah, I'm okay but I need a favor. I need a place to stay for a few days," she said trying not to sound desperate but pretty sure Toni could hear the desperation in her voice.

"I'll tell you what," Toni stopped her, "let me make a call and I'll call you right back. Okay?"

"Okay," Vita said.

Toni made a quick call to Allison, explained that she had a friend that needed to get away and wanted to know if they could stay at the cabin for a few days.

"Sure," Allison said. "That'd be fine."

"Do you need to check with Russ first?" Toni asked, not wanting to be surprised by any of Russ' and Allison's relatives or friends while she and Vita were there.

"I don't need to check with Russ," Allison said kind of annoyed. "You forget, it's my family's cabin, not his!"

Toni laughed a little and let out a sigh of relief and said, "Thanks Allison! Is the spare key in the same spot?"

"Yeah it is. Do you want me to call Sylvia and have her send someone to get it ready for you?"

"That would be great Al! We'll be leaving about three o'clock to beat traffic so should be there about five. I'll call you when we get there. And Al, I owe you," Toni said meaning every word.

The cabin was in the Blue Ridge Mountains in Tennessee, not far from the Georgia state line and only a few hours from Atlanta. Toni had been to the cabin a few times with Allison when she was mad at Russ for something and for an anniversary party she had there a few years ago. It was a nice cabin, modest compared to some of their neighbors' expensive getaways, but it was the perfect place to hide out until the dust settled on this superhero mess. And Toni knew that Allison would make sure the refrigerator was stocked as well as the cabin cleaned.

Toni hung up with Allison and called Vita right back. Ten minutes had elapsed since the first call. Vita answered and Toni told her about the cabin and that it would be the perfect place for them to get away. It was almost one o'clock sharp. Toni told Vita not to pack sheets or towels or anything like that. To only bring clothes, personal items and any gadgets she couldn't live without.

Thanks to one of her sugar daddies, Toni drove a leased four door BMW 3 Series car. She quickly packed her things, locked up her house, stopped by Green's and picked up a twelve pack of Corona light, a 1.5 liter bottle of Tito's vodka, two bottles of champagne and two bottles of Pinot. Vita needed to relax while they were away and whatever she wanted to drink, Toni wanted to be sure she had it. She knew there would be food, juice, soft drinks and water but they were on their own for alcohol. Toni had thought about bringing some weed but decided against it. The last thing she needed would be to get stopped by the police for speeding and getting busted for marijuana possession. The alcohol would do just fine.

Toni arrived at Vita's at two fifty-five and texted her that she was outside and around the back. Vita came down ten minutes later and they took off, heading north on highway I-75 toward Tennessee. Although Toni wanted to help Vita get through her troubles and help her work out a plan of attack, her real motives were to keep Vita away from her own house in case Kristen showed up unexpectedly and also to have sex with her again to gain more of her super powers. The one thing she hadn't figured out yet was the timeframe between having the superpowers transferred into her and extracting the blood quick enough so the superpowers didn't dissipate. One thing Toni was sure of was that at some point over the next few days, she'd have to extract her own blood somehow to store the power for later. The thought of cutting herself on purpose made her sick to her stomach knowing she'd have to cut deep enough to fill a vial of blood. She'd figure something out, she'd have to.

Toni and Vita pulled up to the cottage and Vita commented on how beautiful it was. They gathered everything and went inside. Sylvia's people had done a great job preparing the cottage for their arrival. Fresh flowers in each room, a stocked refrigerator and everything was clean and smelling good like they had just stepped into a luxury suite at the Ritz Carlton. The cabin had three bedrooms but without hesitation they put their things down in the same bedroom. There was no confusion on what the sleeping arrangements would be.

"It's beautiful," Vita said to Toni after they put their things away. "Thanks for bringing me here and getting me out of the city! It's just what I needed." Vita grabbed Toni and gave her a big kiss on the cheek. She then told Toni that she needed to return some calls, that friends had called wanting to make sure she was okay.

"Ok," Toni said. "You can call from there," she said pointing to the deck. "I'll pour us a glass of wine."

While Vita was on the phone Toni texted Kristen who had been blowing her phone up since the newspaper article came out. She was going to call her but she wanted to see how her temperament was first. And it wasn't good. Toni texted, **Hey ... sorry I missed ur calls! Saw article. Call u in a few!**

Toni knew that Kristen was going to grill her about Vita. Kristen had been paying her to find out if she was the superhero and now it was front page news outing her. So if news outlets knew it was Vita, Kristen may start to wonder if she should pay Toni the last half of their agreed upon price. Toni needed to stall to come up with something to tell Kristen but she didn't need Kristen anymore. The knowledge she had was more valuable than any money Kristen could have given her. She certainly wasn't going to tell Kristen about the transference of powers through sex. No, that was her secret and she was going to use that juicy tidbit to her advantage.

Toni was sure that by now Kristen had been by her house, had driven around her block looking for her car and even driven by a few places she knew Toni hung out like the East Lake YMCA, the coffee house on Hosea Williams and her friend's restaurant on Monroe Drive. Knowing she couldn't be found, Toni decided to lie and say she was out of town visiting her sick mother. She hadn't shared much with Kristen about her mother so she wouldn't know if she was lying or not. But what she really thought was, *Fuck Kristen! I don't need her for anything! I have everything I could ever need right here in Tennessee and back in my refrigerator at home.*

Kristen could be unstable so Toni knew she had to call her, so she did. After five minutes of getting cursed out Toni brought up the lie about her sick mother to Kristen, said she had to get off the phone now to care for her mom, that she'd be back in a few days and that they'd get together when she got back. Kristen made it perfectly clear to Toni that she wanted her five hundred dollars back, that if everyone already knew who the superhero was, what good was any info she had?

Toni didn't want Vita to hear her arguing with Kristen and as much as she wanted to curse her out, she kept her composure and took the verbal abuse Kristen heaped onto her. Toni didn't consider herself a violent person but she knew that if Kristen was standing in front of her and talking out of the side of her neck like this at her, she would have slapped her in the mouth. Their conversation ended with Toni hanging up on Kristen. She had had enough. She hung up and turned her phone off.

Vita called her parents to check in, called Tiffanie and told her they'd talk when she got back into town, called Dillon and asked him to water her plants and also told him they'd talk when she got back. She also texted a few other associates who she appreciated had checked in on her. Vita put the phone down after the last text and took a deep breath. She still needed to deactivate her social media accounts but didn't even want to logon to deal with it.

She contemplated how she was going to approach the subject of her superpowers being transferred during kissing and sex with Toni but wasn't sure how to even bring it up. Asking her about it was admitting that she was the superhero and she didn't know Toni well enough to know if she could trust her with this secret. She didn't know what kind of person Toni really was, whether she'd want her to do something illegal with the strength she possessed like rob a bank or break in somewhere and steal something. And what if she denied it? What if she said she hadn't received any superpowers from swapping body fluids? Vita wouldn't be able to prove that Toni was lying but would believe so. Then Vita had the same thought as before; what if her powers were only transferrable to males? Possible, but highly unlikely. She caught herself already making excuses for the lie she knew Toni was going to tell. Another red flag.

When Toni was sure Vita was off the phone, she joined her on the deck. It was a beautiful view, treetop views overlooking houses at the bottom of the hill at the entry of the gated community. She filled Vita's empty wine glass, topped off her own and then sat down.

"So who owns this place?" Vita asked. Toni explained that it belonged to an old friend who had inherited it from her parents when they passed. "It's so peaceful here and so quiet," Vita said. "I hope I can sleep tonight. I'm so used to hearing the freight train and the Marta train going by."

"Don't worry," Toni said. "I'll take care of that!"

They finished the bottle of wine, cooked a nice dinner, cleaned the kitchen together and then relaxed. Vita took a shower in the master bedroom and Toni used the guest bathroom down the hall. Vita finished first and crawled into the king size bed.

"Oh my God," she said out loud as her body sank into the soft, luxurious, high quality cotton sheets. "This must be what Egyptian cotton feels like," she said gleefully to Toni as she came into the room. Vita watched as Toni removed her robe, exposing her subtle breasts, flat stomach, long legs and curvaceous ass. As good as she looked, Vita just wanted to talk. She needed to get to know this woman better, find out where this girl's head was at, where her values were.

Toni climbed in the bed naked and reached for Vita, who pulled back a little. "What's the matter?" Toni asked.

"Nothing. I just want to talk a little. It's been a long day and I thought we could just talk tonight."

Perplexed, Toni moved back to her side of the bed and sat up. Seemingly annoyed, she said, "So, what do you want to talk about?"

"I mean, nothing in particular," Vita softly said wondering if she should have said anything at all. "I just thought maybe you can tell me a little about you, where you're from, where you grew up, how you got to Atlanta? Just regular stuff you ask someone you're dealing with." Vita was curious as to why Toni felt so uncomfortable talking about herself. She wondered what she was hiding. She immediately felt guilty about her questions and her thoughts but she proceeded anyway because this was yet another red flag.

"You know, I've kissed you and even slept with you once and I don't even know your last name."

"So I don't know yours either," Toni snapped. "I also don't know your mother's name, your birthday, your favorite color or whether or not you like getting fucked in the ass!" Seeing the hurt in Vita's face, Toni apologized. She knew she had gone too far and she was sorry.

"Let's talk more tomorrow," Vita said to Toni. "I'm exhausted!" And with that, she reached over, turned off the light and after a few uncomfortable minutes, she fell asleep.

Toni was still awake when she heard Vita snoring lightly. She too had had a trying day and was also exhausted. She turned and looked at sleeping a Vita for a few minutes. She felt that nagging feeling in her stomach again. She felt bad about trying to make money with what she knew about Vita because she really did like her. They got along really well; she was sexy and very good in bed, was a good kisser, had a great sense of humor and seemed to be a genuinely good person. Toni sometimes wished she was more like Vita. She seemed to care about people and was an honest person. And she didn't ever curse. *Who doesn't curse?*

Toni had heard her say a curse word a few times but only when she was really mad or quoting someone. But Toni could only pretend to be like Vita because her background and character makeup was very different. She grew up in a tough neighborhood and learned early on that she had to look out for herself, that she couldn't depend on anyone and the more you expected from people, the more disappointed you'd be each and every time. That's why it was hard for her to trust anyone, get close to anyone or let anyone get close to her. But Vita was different. Toni often daydreamed about being with Vita, really being together but that was a big risk to try that, especially now. She kissed Vita slightly on the cheek, turned off her light and went to sleep.

Kristen was so mad she could barely see straight. How dare Toni hang up on her! That girl didn't know who she was messing with. Kristen tried calling Toni back at least twenty times but no answer. She cursed Toni out over text, then apologized but still no response. "Fuck you!" Kristen yelled out loud to no one over and over again. If anyone was watching her they would have thought she was crazy.

Knowing Toni was not around, Kristen drove to her neighborhood, parked her car around the corner and nonchalantly went around the back of her duplex and tried looking through the windows but the blinds were down and she couldn't see anything. Then she tried the backdoor but it was locked, she pretended to knock on the front door while trying to sneakily look and feel around for a spare key. One of Toni's neighbors walked out to her mailbox and yelled to Kristen that she didn't think Toni was home and she told her that she'd seen her leaving earlier with a few bags like she was going out of town. Kristen figured maybe Toni was telling the truth about visiting her sick mother after all. Suddenly she felt guilty about what she was doing and left. She'd have to do a lot of apologizing when Toni did return because of those ugly text messages and voicemails she left. She'd left so many messages that Toni's voicemail was full.

Although her initial reason for befriending Toni was to get someone next to Vita to find out if she was the superhero, she had begun to have real feelings for Toni. She was going to have to return to California soon and thought about asking Toni to move out there with her. Kristen knew Toni didn't have the same romantic feelings for her but

Kristen believed she may have had a
chance since the only person Toni cared
about was Toni and the fact that she was
a taker, more interested in what she
could get from you than give to you,
made Kristen feel that she had a chance.
It was a risk but Toni seemed to be an
opportunist who was driven by money
and what she could get for herself, which
made Kristen feel confident that Toni
might accept her offer. Kristen secretly
hoped so.

By the time Toni woke up, Vita was
already up and out of the house. Toni
looked around and noticed her sneakers
were gone so she assumed Vita had gone
for a walk or a run. There were some
nice trails leading up the mountains and
if Vita had woken her up, she would
have joined her. Toni got up, made
coffee and ate a little breakfast. She then
sat on the front porch taking in the
beautiful scenery and waited for Vita to
return.

Ninety minutes later Vita came
walking up the gravel driveway. "Good

morning," she yelled out to Toni a few yards before she got to the front porch.

"Why didn't you wake me before you left?" Toni asked. "I would have gone sightseeing with you."

"You were sleeping so peacefully that I didn't want to wake you."

"So where did you go, running?" Toni was taken aback by how her own question came out. It sounded more suspicious or jealous or like she was angry that she wasn't invited.

Vita stared at her for a few seconds before answering. "I started out running a few trails and then ran into a group going hiking up one of the larger mountains and they invited me to come along." Vita described her hike, the trails and the great snacks they shared with her. "As a matter of fact, the Mitchells, who live two houses over, invited us to dinner tonight. They know your friend Allison and they're having a few friends over tonight and invited us. Want to go? I think it'll be fun," Vita said.

"Aren't you concerned about the superhero thing? I thought we came up her to hide," Toni asked.

"The group already asked me about that when I first met them on the trail. I told them that everybody thinks that I'm her but that I wasn't. They joked that she must be my long lost twin then," Vita explained. She continued,

"I'll just keep deflecting until they get tired of asking. And besides," she added, "we'll only be here a few more days and I'll probably never see them again anyway, so who cares? I'm going to take a shower," Vita said as she hustled past Toni.

Vita rang the Mitchell's doorbell. Sandra, the woman who had invited her to go hiking with them, answered the door and greeted them both with hugs. Toni handed over the M5 bottle of wine from Allison's wine cellar. The one time she and Allison had fooled around was after drinking a bottle and a half of it and it quickly became one of Toni's favorites, a wine blended with five grapes that Allison and her family had shipped in by the caseloads from the Margerum Wine Company in Santa Barbara.

"Thank you so much," Sandra said, welcoming the two of them into her home.

The dinner was delicious, a choice of chicken or pork loin with homemade mashed potatoes, steamed green beans with an apple-cherry chutney, a dish similar to a peach cobbler without the bottom or top crust and not so sweet so it was eaten as a side dish rather than a dessert. There were also plenty of other wines to choose from, hard liquor and beer. Someone even brought homemade Sangria. Vita enjoyed sitting around the large table, everyone sharing stories and laughing. There were six other people there, most married and older.

One of the older gentlemen was telling a story about how he met his wife while in college when suddenly he stood up and grabbed his throat. His wife started asking if he was okay and everyone was saying, "What's going on?" Everyone thought he was having a heart attack but he wasn't talking, he wasn't making any sounds at all.

All of a sudden his wife yelled, "Oh my God, he's choking!"

The man was extremely overweight, probably weighing three hundred pounds or more. Everyone knew the proper thing to do was the Heimlich Maneuver but none of them was large enough to wrap their arms around him in an attempt to clear the blockage.

Vita felt a little irritation on her stomach but not the full heat of burning she had felt the other times people were in danger and needed her help. She calmly walked over to the man and grabbed his hand. She first tried performing back blows to dislodge whatever he was choking on but when that didn't work she quickly moved to abdominal thrusts.

She pulled him towards her as she went and stood in front of a dining room wall. She stood with her back against the wall, placed her left arm as far around the man's stomach as she could, and as fast and as hard as she could, reached around and with her fist punched the man just above the navel but under his breastbone. The force was so strong she was barely able to keep him on his feet with her other hand. At first nothing happened but on the third try the piece of chicken was dislodged and it flew a few feet in the air before landing on the other side of the room. The man started coughing; it was a few scary moments before his breathing returned to normal. When Vita moved everyone began to stare. Not at her but at the hole in the wall she had made while helping the chocking man.

When everyone turned their attention back to the chocking man, Toni grabbed Vita and pulled her into the kitchen. Seizing her opportunity to get some of Vita's powers transferred to her, she quickly kissed her, opened mouthed.

"What are you doing?" Vita said pulling away.

"I'm sorry honey," Toni started. "That was so amazing! You were so brave saving that man's life like that. I'm just so proud of you!"

"Ok but that's a very weird way of showing that you're proud. Let's get back in there and make sure he's doing okay," Vita said making her way back into the living room.

When they returned the man's wife came over and gave Vita a bear hug and said she couldn't thank her enough for saving her husband's life. Everyone else was cheering Vita on, toasting her for such quick thinking and level headedness. Meanwhile, while everyone was showering Vita with praises, Toni was testing her theory that Vita's powers were only transferrable after a lifesaving episode. And to test it she picked up a silver spoon and easily bent it in half. She smiled. She then tried something bigger, a stainless steel spatula she found in the utensil drawer but was unable to bend it no matter how hard she tried. *Ok,* she thought. *Since that wasn't full blown superwoman superhero, the power transference was slight. No need to draw blood for this tiny amount. It's not worth the risk.* She'd wait for the next big episode and then she'd have enough blood to sell to the highest bidder! The rest of their vacation served up only relaxation and calm days.

Things quieted down for Vita and Atlanta over the next few days. The superwoman story was replaced by the domestic abuse scandal that rocked the National Football League and the nation and also by the ongoing war in Syria. So after three fun-filled days of drinking, Netflix, long baths, great dinners and lots of laughs, Vita and Toni headed back to the city. It was eight on a Thursday night when Toni dropped Vita off, gave her a hug and a little kiss and went home.

She pulled into her driveway and got out but while walking up to her front door she noticed things around her front door had been moved or were slightly disturbed. Before going in she walked around to the back door but it was secure, then checked her windows and everything was fine there too. *Odd*. Toni went inside.

Reluctantly she turned on her phone. There were screens and screens of text messages from Kristen, a few from the two guys she was seeing, one from Allison checking to make sure everything was okay at the cottage and at least twenty-five voicemails from Kristen. Without listening or reading any of Kristen's text messages, she deleted them all. Toni checked her email and quickly called back both her male clients, telling them she was out of town looking after her sick mother, that she missed them and that they'd get together as soon as she was back in town in a few weeks. She checked the bag of potatoes and made sure the blood vials were still there, opened a bottle of wine and took a shower. Although the cottage was beautiful and comfortable and being there with Vita was an added bonus, it was nice to be home, to sleep in her own bed so close to the jackpot stored in her fridge.

Vita woke up early Friday morning also glad to be home. She texted Tiffanie and told her to come by after work for dinner and to catch up. She hadn't seen her since the party when she had to drive her home and she felt guilty about not making time for her friend. Tiffanie accepted the invitation and texted that she'd be there by six. **Perfect**, Vita texted back. **See you then!** Vita went to the store and bought the fixings for a spaghetti dinner and side salad, since she was on an extremely tight budget. Her apartment wasn't that messy so cleaning only took an hour. She took a shower, changed and started dinner. Tiffanie arrived a few minutes before six which was fine because everything was ready.

She and Vita hugged and talked about how long it had been since they had seen each other. Tiffanie was dating a new guy and started telling Vita all the drama about him and his family, how she thought he was cheating on her but how fine he was and how the sex was and that she knew she should leave him but she couldn't and on and on and on. It was nice to talk about something other than her superhero problems.

"Want to see a picture of him?" Tiffanie asked as she got up to get another glass of wine. "And I want to show you some pics of my friend's going away party hosted by my company that I invited you to, but you missed! You should have come. It was open bar all night!" Tiffanie pulled out her phone to show Vita what she missed.

She was flipping through the pictures of the party when Vita saw someone familiar. "Hold up, go back."

Tiffanie swiped back a few pictures until Vita said stop. The look on her face made Tiffanie ask her what was wrong. "See somebody you know?"

"Yeah, I do," Vita said. "Remember her?" She said pointing to a picture of Toni. "She was at the party where we saw each other last." But the shocked look on Vita's face wasn't because Toni was at Tiffanie's company party. Obviously they would have some friends in common. It was because of who Toni was with. Although she was a little older, Vita recognized her immediately. It was Kristen! And there she was in Atlanta and in the background of the picture hugged up with Toni!

"You sure you're okay?" Tiffanie asked. "You look like you've just seen a ghost!" Tiffanie asked Vita if she had any history with the woman in the picture and Vita told Tiffanie about the tire incident, being knocked in the head at the club and the broken car window. Then she continued about how she always thought that Kristen was behind all of it and it only stopped when the crazy fool moved to California for a new job. She also told her about the one time they hooked up and how Kristen sort of stalked her, calling and texting all the time, begging her to go out and how she finally had to tell her that it wasn't going to happen again and that she didn't like her like that.

"I guess she didn't take it very well, did she?" Tiffanie said as they both laughed hysterically.

"I guess not," Vita said still laughing. They continued laughing about Kristen and the more they drank, the funnier they thought everything was.

Vita was glad she could laugh like this now because it had taken her years to feel secure and not look over her shoulder everywhere she went. And she knew it was no coincidence that her so called "bad luck" ended as soon as Kristen left town.

I guess it's possible for Kristen and Toni to know each other, Vita thought and she couldn't think of any conversation she and Toni had where it would have ever come up. But somehow she couldn't shake the feeling that there was more to this story than casual friends meeting out, having a drink. Way more.

Instinctively, Vita checked her phone during a Tiffanie bathroom break. She hadn't spoken with Toni all day and she had not received any text messages and no voicemails from her either. *She probably had to check in with all the people she didn't call while we were away.* And she was cool with it. After Toni snapped on her the first night they arrived when she was trying to find out more about Toni's background, she had taken a few steps back. They hadn't slept together while they were there either. Toni had tried but Vita let her know that her advances were unwelcomed until they got to know each other better. And the only kiss was the one Toni had given her after she had saved the choking man's life. Still, whenever Toni didn't call or text, Vita found herself thinking about her more.

It was Vita's *modus operandi* to be attracted to people who posed a challenge. She wasn't attracted to those who she could walk all over, who said yes to any and everything, who never snapped or got mad at her or even cursed at her a little. And the less attracted to her they seemed, the more she was attracted to them. It was part of human nature, she knew it was and also knew she should work on breaking out of that pattern in the future. She was mostly attracted to people who were self-confident, almost to the point of being arrogant, a little cocky, positive self-image, high self-esteem; someone who believed in their own abilities and someone who knew how to laugh and have a good time.

Vita wanted to send a **"thinking about you"** text but knew how pathetic that sounded. **"Hope you're having a good day"** sounded just as bad. She wanted to say something without revealing too much about how she was feeling. After texting and deleting a few cutesy phrases she decided to send nothing. "Fuck her," she said out loud to no one. She didn't really feel that way but the wine was kicking in and Vita was feeling a little full of herself.

Vita and Tiffanie drank two bottles of wine and both of them were drunk. Tiffanie slept over on the couch. It was a good night for both of them. Vita got to let her hair down and catch up with a friend she had been missing for a long time. The nicest part of the night was that they didn't bring up the media speculation about Vita being the superhero. If Tiffanie had thought about bringing it up, she didn't. She knew the media attention, online, local and national news outlets were the reason Vita had left town for a few days after the front page article came out and were the reasons she was fired. They were just being friends, and it was so nice to just hang out.

Toni got up around seven-thirty and called Sugar Daddy Number One. She agreed to meet him for lunch at twelve-thirty; meaning sex in his office. She called Sugar Daddy Number Two and agreed to meet him for drinks after work which meant sex with him in the bathroom of the bar or restaurant they went to or in his car.

In preparation for her work, she scheduled an appointment at Mandarin Oriental in Buckhead for a massage, manicure, pedicure and bikini and leg wax. There wasn't enough time to get her hair done but she wore it low in a stylish Mohawk which always looked good. She could use a cut but she knew she still looked good enough for the day and night ahead. She picked out an outfit for lunch with Sugar Daddy Number One. He liked her dressed ultra-feminine, tight fitting dress and high heels. Sugar Daddy Number Two liked the more masculine look, tailored pants suit and high heels. But both had the same taste when it came to what she wore under her clothes, low-rise, lace front and sheer mesh panties with a garter belt and matching push up bra.

For lunch Toni decided on a cotton, grey linen skirt slit high over one thigh and paired it with a light blue button-front oxford blouse with blue stripes of different widths on the collar, pockets and sleeves positioned close together. For shoes she chose her suede and fabric Manolo Blahnik pumps Sugar Daddy Number One had bought her on one of their weekend trips to New York. And for dinner she picked out a wide-legged trouser with a cropped top, a lightweight leopard coat and yellow bag. She would wear the same shoes. There wouldn't be enough time to run home after lunch, shower, dress and head out again for an early dinner and an hour or so of sex with Sugar Daddy Number Two, so Toni packed a bag containing her dinner outfit and accessories. She then got dressed, grabbed her new leather bag and sun glasses, took a look around and headed out the door.

Toni pulled up to the Four Seasons Hotel, tossed her keys to the valet and walked through the hotel lobby to the restaurant. Number One was already seated at a table towards the back and he stood up and kissed her on the cheek when she got to the table.

"You look beautiful darling," he said, slipping his hand from the small of her back to her ass.

"Thank you. You know I always want to look good for you."

They both ordered a cocktail and then lunch: grilled Dover sole with a side salad for her, prime rib and mixed vegetables for him. Toni spoke about her fake trip to visit her sick mother and although Number One tried to feign interest in what she was saying, Toni was sure his thoughts were purely on the suite he had reserved upstairs.

The ritual was the same each time. They'd meet for lunch at the Four Seasons Hotel or some other upscale hotel, have lunch at the restaurant and then head to the suite after lunch for a few minutes of actual sex but many relaxing hours of bubble baths, champagne, room service and sometimes an overnight stay for her. He never spent more than an hour or two in the suite with Toni but let her enjoy it and stay as long as she wanted. He also knew that Toni dated women so all she ever had to say was that she wanted to invite a girlfriend over later and he would book the suite for the night. She knew the staff kept tabs on her visitors and probably reported back to him; so she kept it to women only. The thought of two beautiful women having sex, taking baths together, showering and romping around in a room he paid for was a turn on for him and Toni was grateful for his generosity.

This day was no different. At exactly one thirty they were headed upstairs. Number One liked to sit in a chair and watch her undress, hence the sexy lingerie. Then while still in her lingerie, garter belt and high heels, he liked her to remove her shoes, then straddle him and slowly remove his tie and unbutton his shirt, then loosen his belt and slowly unzip his pants. Then he would pick her up, drop her on the king sized bed, remove her bra and suck on her breasts. The actual sex act took all of ten minutes and then he was done. Ten minutes for three thousand dollars a month, Toni could do that all day. Right before the end of each month he would give her the money in cash for her rent, car, utilities and for whatever else she needed money.

"I'm meeting a friend for drinks at five so I'm going to hang round a little longer," Toni called into the bathroom to him after their romp.

"That's fine dear," was the only response she got. He was dressed in a few minutes, looking exactly as he did in the restaurant. He told Toni he was going on a family vacation in three weeks but would call her as soon as he returned. "I put a little extra in this month in case you need anything while I'm away," he said grabbing his keys.

"Thank you," Toni said, wrapping her arms around his neck and kissing him on the cheek.

"I'll see ya kid," Number One said as he left the suite.

Toni looked over at the night table and picked up the envelope and counted the cash. "Thirty-five hundred," she said out loud. "Not bad. Not bad at all!"

Time to get ready for Number Two.

Toni usually didn't see both guys in the same day but it was close to the end of the month and she had been away so she had to do what she needed to do. Not that it would really be hard on her. Sal, Sugar Daddy Number Two, was younger, wealthier and harder to please than Number One. Toni actually had to work for the money she got from him.

He gave her thirty-five hundred dollars a month to also pay her rent, car note, utilities and other things she needed to buy to which she had become accustomed. He was half Italian and half Puerto Rican, six feet tall, slightly overweight but trying to keep it together and a hell of a lot of fun.

They met at a new spot on Edgewood for tapas, live music and dancing. Occasionally they went to stuffy, sit-down, fancy restaurants in Buckhead but Sal liked the bars and clubs in the trendy, in-town neighborhoods like Inman Park, Old Fourth Ward, Oakhurst, East Atlanta, Kirkwood and Candler Park. He was a snob about the Northeast side. Toni did her best to try and get him to the Westside of town but to no avail. When Sal found a place or area of town he liked, it was almost impossible to get him to try anything else.

He had already had two margaritas by the time she got there, so he was overly affectionate and very touchy-feely but Toni didn't mind. She liked Sal and liked being out with him. They made an attractive couple and he could relax and be himself because none of his family, friends or business associates would ever patronize a place like the one where they were. Sal was married with four children. He told Toni that he loved his wife but needed a little something else. Toni never asked how many women he had on the side because she didn't care. As long as he took care of her and treated her well, she didn't care about anything else.

While waiting on their food, Sal said, "You been following the stories about that woman superhero who's been all in the news? She is so fucking hot! I'd love to fuck her," he said, barely catching his breath. Toni just stared at him, not saying anything. "What?" he said.

"Nothing. I'm just listening to you," she said.

"What, you don't think she's hot?" Sal asked. "I know you do. I know you better than you think," Sal said.

Toni could tell that Sal was getting drunk so she just let him keep talking. Secretly she hoped he would write her a larger check, which he usually did when he was drunk.

"If I was her and had her superpowers, I'd rob a bank or something," Sal said. "Or better yet, I'd rob my cousin Vinny!"

Toni's ears perked up paying attention to what Sal was saying. "Why would you rob your own cousin?" Toni asked trying not to sound too interested.

"Because he's a drug dealer and owns a car wash and a nail salon which are both fronts for his illegal drug business."

Toni didn't say anything. She didn't want to appear too anxious or too interested, but was *very* interested. Sal had never spoken of his family besides his wife and kids to her. She didn't know he had a drug dealing cousin living in Atlanta.

"And I'd rob him on Sunday night," Sal continued with delightfully slurred speech. "I know for a fact that he doesn't make his cash deposits until Monday mornings. He's got three small banks he launders his money through and those banks are all closed on weekends!"

Toni continued trying to look disinterested although a light bulb went off in her head. Before she even had a chance to talk herself out of the direction her mind was quickly moving to, the plan was already formulated.

Sal was drunk and had moved on to another topic. He was babbling on about something but all Toni could think about was the cash at Sal's cousin's businesses. Somehow she needed to get Sal back on that topic and find out where the businesses were located, where the cash was kept and if there were cameras and a security system.

"Come on, let's get out of here," Toni said whispering in Sal's ear and sticking her breasts in his face. "I've missed you and want you now," she added. She knew that would get him up, now all she had to do was to get him talking again. They left the restaurant and waited for the car.

When the valet brought the car around, Sal said, "Where to little lady?"

They were close to her apartment so Toni told him they could go to her place. She had dropped her car off at her apartment and taken Uber to meet Sal and he was drunk so she drove his car.

Sal was also different than Number One in that way too, there was no schedule, no place they always went to when they were together. Sometimes they had sex in his office, sometimes in his car, many times at her apartment; whenever and wherever the mood struck them. Sal was all over Toni as she pulled into the driveway. He was grinding on her ass and groping her breasts as she opened the front door. They went straight to her bedroom, pulled off their clothes and Toni grabbed a condom from her night table. Sal was lying on his back and Toni straddled him, keeping on her high heels. But there was some business to take care of first so Toni dove right in.

"You know I was really turned on hearing you say how you would rob your cousin Vincent. Tell me more about how you'd do it. How would you get past the security system and how do you know where they keep the money? Gangster is hot. Talk to me," she said in as sexy a voice as she could muster.

She brought the condom up to her lips and tore it open. Sal began talking, anticipating the great sex he was about to have. Toni worked Sal like he was a job, giving a little sex when she got the information she wanted and holding up when she needed more. By the end of their session she had gotten exactly what she needed: the hours and location of both businesses, the fact that the security systems in both businesses were being replaced next weekend and that on any given Sunday there was at least three hundred thousand dollars between the two locations. Toni threw in a second quick fuck after hearing the dollar amount. She expected a few thousand dollars but not that much and it was obvious Sal had taken a Viagra or some erectile dysfunction pill so he wasn't in any rush to leave.

Sal finally left an hour later. It was still early so Toni ran a bath. She added lots of bubble bath, lit all the candles in the bathroom and made herself a large, strong margarita with Patron. Her mind was racing with excitement knowing in a few days she'd be hundreds of thousands of dollars

richer than she was today. She'd have to
do her research though, verify their
hours of operation, when the last
employee left the building and somehow
get a look at the layout of each location.
Another unknown was the potency of
the blood samples stored in her
refrigerator. The perfect scenario would
be for her to test the blood first but with
so little of it, she didn't want to waste
any. She was just going to have to risk it,
inject herself with one of the vials and
hope she had enough strength and
power to get in, open the safes and get
out fast!

Toni was about to step into her
steaming bubble bath when she thought
she heard something outside the
bathroom window. She put her bathrobe
back on, walked through the kitchen and
looked out the back door. She didn't see
anything but opened the door and
walked outside and looked around just
to be sure. Not seeing anyone or any
animals around, she went back inside.

She had walked right by Kristen
hiding behind the recycle bin.

Once inside, Toni made sure she
locked the back door, she checked all the
locks on her windows and checked the
front door. When she was satisfied that
all was secure, she checked her most
prized possession again; the blood vials
in the fridge. They were also safe but she

couldn't resist the urge to hold a vial in her hand to feel the power that would soon be coursing through her body.

Unfortunately for her though, Kristen had been peering through the kitchen window and saw her remove the vials of blood from the hole in the potato. Kristen didn't know what she was looking at but she knew it was something special the way Toni was holding one of the vials.

"Interesting," Kristen whispered. "I wonder what that's all about." Kristen knew somehow she was going to have to break into Toni's apartment and get those hidden vials. *But how?*

Vita called Toni the next morning and invited her to lunch. They hadn't seen each other in a few days and if Vita was honest with herself, she missed her despite the red flags. They met at one, then went back to Vita's and sat on the patio and people-watched a little. They went to the movies that night and Toni didn't leave until one in the morning. And they saw each other for the next four days and three nights in a row. They laughed, held hands, kissed affectionately whenever they got the chance, stared at each other when they thought the other one wasn't looking and enjoyed their simple time together.

Vita thought about confronting Toni about Kristen but didn't know how to bring it up and she didn't want Toni lying or getting mad again like she did at the cottage when Vita tried asking her all the questions about upbringing and her past. Vita had learned quickly that Toni had a short temper and everything was going so well with them that she didn't want to ruin it.

They were inseparable. Dillon had been texting her to see if she was hungry and wanted some food, Tiffanie called her a few times inviting her to a few company drinking functions but she declined all requests. The only person she wanted to spend time with right now was Toni.

"So what do you want to do this weekend?" Vita asked Toni as they were cooking dinner at Vita's apartment one Wednesday night.

Hesitantly and with as much sensitivity as she could muster, Toni said, "I have plans this weekend with an old friend that I made with weeks ago; I can't get out of them I'm afraid." This was the weekend Toni was breaking into Sal's cousin's businesses to steal his drug money. "But it's only Sunday so we can do something on Monday, Tuesday, Wednesday..." Toni said as she walked towards Vita and began kissing her.

Saturday morning Toni mapped her routes first to the nail salon which was on the south side of town in the

hood, off Fulton Industrial Boulevard
and then the car wash located off of
Candler Road in Decatur. Decatur was
closest so she headed there first.

She parked nearby to get a look at
visible security cameras from
neighboring businesses but didn't see
any. There were plenty of stores that
tried to give the appearance of a security
camera but with her binoculars she
could see they all had cracked lenses,
wires that were dangling and not
connected to anything or they were
pointed upward to the sky. *No problem
here.* She'd have to come back at night
to see the atmosphere after hours and to
see the security that was put around the
building. There was a chain link fence
with barbed wire across the top going all
around the car wash so either she'd have
to cut through it or go over it. But she
was pretty confident she'd cased the
outside security situation thoroughly.

Next she got behind the line of
cars already waiting to get her car
washed. She was asked what service she
wanted and then as she drove closer to
the actual car wash machines, another
attendant gave her a ticket, took her
keys and pointed her towards the office
to pay and wait for her car. The inside
was unassuming, a clerk taking tickets
and cash, credit or debit card payments,
a customer bathroom, a small lobby with

a cheap flat screen television on the wall and eight guest chairs. When she walked up to the counter to pay, she noticed one security camera in the corner pointed directly at the cash register and another in the lobby. Toni asked what time they closed and the girl behind the counter said they closed at six on weekends. Continuing to look around, Toni noticed a door marked Employees Only where she assumed the safe probably was and that was it.

The car wash was shitty but it was only twenty dollars for a hand wash so customers got what they paid for. Next she headed to Fulton Industrial to get a manicure at the nail salon. Once outside, she repeated her steps, checked for security cameras outside of the business location, went inside and got a look at security and layout of the inside. Again, no problem from what she saw but she'd be back at night to see the outside security.

Toni headed back to both locations at ten that night. When she got back to the car wash, the front gates were pulled closed with a humungous padlock on the thick chain plus there was barbed wire at the top just like the fence surrounding the entire car wash. The nail salon had one of those pull down aluminum security doors on the front door and Toni assumed on the back door too. *But that won't be a problem.* With superpowers, she'd be in and out in a flash.

Now that the homework was out of the way, the next step was to shop for the supplies she needed for tomorrow night. She went to Target and purchased a large gym bag big enough to hold three hundred thousand dollars. She already had black leggings, a black hoodie and black sneakers. She stopped by The Home Depot on Ponce and bought a pair of bolt cutters, just in case she needed to cut the fence. Her last stop was the beauty supply store where she picked up a dark brown, long haired wig before heading home to plan out her heist step by step. Tomorrow was the night and she was feeling a little nervous but when she thought about the money and how her life would change, she quickly got over it. The unknown element in her plan was whether the blood vials had held their potency but she couldn't test them because she didn't want to waste a drop. Although it was risky, she was just going to have to trust that everything would work out.

Toni barely slept Saturday night. She was up early Sunday morning and knew she needed to burn off the excited energy. She cleaned her apartment from top to bottom, vacuumed and mopped the floors, washed and folded laundry;

she even cleaned the oven and refrigerator. She thought about washing her car but decided against that as she didn't want to attract any unwanted attention.

It was still early afternoon so she went to the gym and worked out for an hour. When she was completely spent, she returned home. It was only six; she still had three hours until she was going to leave. Luckily it had started raining really hard, which was great, because that meant no foot traffic and less traffic period. At eight she began getting dressed. She was still excited about the money but she was also excited about the superpowers she was about to have. She put on a shiny pair of purple leggings, her thigh high boots and a tight black sleeveless shirt. She went into the kitchen and picked up the blood vial that was sitting on the table, held it up to the light and stared at it.

"I hope you're still powerful enough to do the trick," she said out loud. She then grabbed one of her skinny leather belts, tied it around her upper left arm, filled a syringe with the blood from the vial and injected it into the large vein in the middle of her arm.

Afterwards she didn't know what to expect so she sat there for a minute not knowing if she was going to be overcome with a feeling of a sudden rush like if she had just shot heroin or something. In fact, Toni had no idea what shooting heroin actually felt like. She was going by how it looked in the movies or on television when someone shot up, how their whole body seemed to stiffen, then relax suddenly as a warm looking feeling overtook them. She waited a few minutes but felt nothing. Disappointed, she went into her bedroom and grabbed the bat she kept under her bed for protection, held it up and easily snapped it in two.

"Yes," she yelled out loud. "It works!" Although she had hoped it would work, she couldn't believe it actually worked! She now had some of the same powers Vita had. And now all she had to do was finish dressing like her and she'd be ready to go. She put on black gloves and a black leather jacket. And the *pièce de résistance*, the long, dark brown wig. She put it on and looked in the mirror. Toni was taken aback by what she saw. If she didn't know it was herself, she would have sworn she was the superhero! And she was proud of her accomplishment, proud that she had taken the time to get every little detail correct and now she was her, she was the superhero!

Toni grabbed her black duffle bag which held the bolt cutters, flashlight, gloves, knife and pepper spray. She also brought the other vial of blood, the belt and syringe just in case her powers wore off before she was able to rob both locations. It was time to go. Toni took one more look at herself in the mirror and headed out the door.

Two hours later she was back in her apartment and hopefully three hundred thousand dollars richer. She hadn't needed the second vial of blood so she returned it to its hiding place in the refrigerator. Then she poured herself a shot of Colonel E.H. Taylor's Barrel Proof bourbon. This was expensive shit that she only broke out for hard core bourbon drinkers when she wanted to impress them. But thought she deserved it for pulling off such a daring heist, but mostly she needed it to calm her nerves now that all the excitement was over. She just couldn't stop shaking no matter how hard she tried to relax.

She figured if Vincent was going to report the theft it would be sometime on Monday after he strategized how to explain to the police that his drug earnings were stolen. Toni poured herself another shot of bourbon. She also couldn't stop her mind from racing and thinking of all the different scenarios of what could go wrong. This wasn't the first time she had robbed someone. She and her friends routinely stole from stores when they were young and once robbed a neighborhood store, pretending to have a gun in their pocket. They only got a few hundred dollars but the rush she felt then was exactly what she was feeling now.

She was so full of herself and cocky at that moment, she didn't know what to do with herself. Then she remembered she hadn't counted the money yet. Toni started streaming WCLK on her phone because she needed to hear something calming and the sounds of jazz was exactly what she needed. Toni then dumped the duffle bag filled with money onto her bedroom floor and stood there frozen, just staring at it. It was so much. When she was stealing it she kept reaching into both safes and shoving as much as she could, as fast as she could in the bag. The cash was in all different denominations, all different serial numbers with new mixed with old. "The perfect score," Toni said out loud. She didn't yell, she didn't want to wake up her neighbors or bring any unwanted attention to herself, but she wanted to holler and dance around.

She stacked the money by denomination in piles of one hundred. She started out placing the money piles on the floor but quickly realized she'd run out of floor space before she was even half of the way done counting. It was that much money!

"Holy shit," she said, moving furniture around to make even more floor space. Toni took a break when she got to one hundred thousand dollars. Sal wasn't lying when he said there'd be a lot of money in the safes over the weekend. She kept counting. She soon ran out of floor space so she put separators in between the first hundred thousand and stacked another thousand on top of those piles. Again she paused when she got to two hundred thousand. There looked to be about another fifty thousand or so left to count. It was three o'clock in the morning and she had been counting money for three and a half hours. In all her planning wisdom, she forgot to pick up a money counter. *Stupid me*, she thought. Her fingers were all raw, chapped and cut at the tips from counting and her back was aching from all the bending over. She could really use one of Vita's masterful massages right about now. She poured another bourbon shot. She drank half the bottle and wasn't close to being drunk. She was still too excited to get drunk but it did help to calm her nerves. An hour and a half later she finished counting with a final tally being two hundred eighty-three thousand dollars. "My life will never be the same," Toni said aloud but quietly. Exhausted, she took a quick shower and fell onto her bed leaving the stacks of money exactly where they were. She was fast asleep within minutes.

Vinny's cell phone woke him at six-forty Monday morning. Due to the time, he knew it was going to be bad news as soon as he answered it. The voice on the other end told him the car wash had been robbed, that the fence was intact so the perp must have gone over it, that the doorknob and lock on the back door had been broken like someone had just torn them off and that the safe was empty. He described the safe as having a big hole in the middle of it where someone had taken a hammer or something and beat a hole in it and took all the money that was in there. Vincent knew it was trouble for him by then. He had installed a security camera inside the safe that was still working last night. The security company had disabled the cameras in his other businesses but Vincent thought he'd be protected as long as his money was safe from robbers. And if he did get robbed, he'd have a good look at the

criminals and would deal with them his
way. Now all he'd have is a hand
reaching through a hole in his safe
stealing his hard earned drug money.

He told the voice on the other end
to sit tight and that he'd call him back in
a few minutes. Vinny's next call was to
his brother. He told him what happened
at the carwash and told him to get down
to the nail salon and make sure things
were okay there. His brother called him
back thirty minutes later with bad news;
the nail salon had also been robbed. He
described the condition of the safe—the
same as the safe at the carwash, a big
hole in the middle and all the money
gone!

The employees at the nail salon
didn't know their business was used as a
money laundering business for Vinny's
drug running carwash. Along with car
washes, customers also ordered weed,
coke, Oxycodone, OxyContin, Adderall,
meth and the biggest seller of all, heroin.

Vinny called the other managers
of the nail salon and carwash and told
them to meet him at the carwash at ten
o'clock sharp. He didn't care if it was
their day off, he wanted them all there.
Once everyone gathered, he grilled them
on their whereabouts, the whereabouts
of their staff and anyone who was acting
suspicious the last few days or anyone
who had suddenly gone missing. But

everyone's whereabouts and movements the previous night had been accounted for. Everyone had an alibi ... airtight alibis.

Next Vinny called Sal and told him what happened and asked if he had mentioned to anyone that he was changing out his security system over the weekend. Sal lied and said no, that he hadn't mentioned it to anyone. After Vinny described the way the money was stolen, Sal immediately dismissed Toni as having anything to do with the robberies because she didn't have the strength to put a hole in a safe but then again, maybe she told someone. Sal asked Vinny what he was going to do and Vinny replied that he didn't know yet.

"Fucking cunt," Sal yelled out in his three car garage after he hung up. Even if he suspected Toni, no way was he ever going to mention to Vinny that he even knew her.

Next Vinny organized his troops and they went door to door asking all their neighboring businesses if they had functioning exterior cameras. Most said no but some said yes. After reviewing hours of video from businesses located around the carwash and hair salon, they came across one store owner who had installed cameras across the street from the carwash on the side of an abandoned building. Amazingly, it had a clear view of the back of the carwash and the view was wide enough to see the perpetrator jumping the side fence before making their way to the back door. What they saw left them speechless. The thief walked from the darkness to the right side of the building, looked around and literally hopped over the fence. Their eight foot fence ... just jumped right over it. Then they crept to the back door, knowing exactly where it was, gripped the back door handle and tore it off. Literally ripped it right off of its hinges. The next thing the video showed was the thief coming out with a heavy looking duffle bag, throwing it over the fence, hopping back over and disappearing around the corner.

The one thing that was clear to those who saw the video was that the thief was a woman who bore a striking resemblance to the superhero woman who was in the news about two weeks ago. The same woman who saved kidnapped children and people from burning buildings, toppled cars and fires. It was the same woman jumping over the fence and stealing the money!

Instead of going to the cops, Vinny leaked the story to a news reporter he had in his pocket who then ran the story on the local evening news Monday night. In fact, all the local news channels began with the same story, "Hometown Superhero Turns Criminal." The stories told of the woman superhero's recent financial difficulties after getting fired from her job. They painted a picture of her going from good to evil, rich to poor, employed to homeless. Most of the information the stories reported was pure fabrication but that didn't stop the media from once again perching themselves outside of Vita's apartment building.

Vita had gone for a run and was almost at the end of her third mile when her phone started ringing, one call after the other along with text messages. She ignored them at first but then thought there must be an emergency. She stopped running, sat on a nearby bench and watched a video one of her friends sent her. Her jaw dropped when she saw it! If she didn't know any better she would have sworn she was watching herself jump over a fence, break into a back door and emerge with a duffle bag, throw it over the same fence and disappear into the night. Stunned she started the video again and zoomed in. The woman bore a striking resemblance to her: same hair, outfit, boots, coat and superpowers. The only problem was that Vita knew that wasn't her. But proving it would be another story. She was home alone last night catching up on television

shows she had taped and watching a
Law & Order marathon. She didn't
remember talking to or texting anyone
but checked her phone just to be sure.
So not only was Vita going to have to
prove she didn't rob those businesses,
she was somehow going to have to prove
that she was home at the time of the
robberies.

Scared at the thought of being
thrown in jail for something she didn't
do, Vita knew her best bet was to get an
attorney but unfortunately she couldn't
afford one. And it was only a matter of
time before the police came knocking on
her door. Everyone was checking in with
her to make sure she was okay. And
although no one said it, Vita knew that
despite her denials, they all believed she
was the superhero. Otherwise, why
check in with her now? But interestingly
enough, the only person who hadn't
checked in was Toni.

Monday came and went with no
visit from the police. The woman
superhero was again trending on Twitter
and there were too many comments to
read on the Facebook fan page someone
created after the first rescue. Vita was
still nervous but by Wednesday night the
police still hadn't knocked on her door.
Her friend Tiffanie had a friend who
worked in the dispatch department of
the Atlanta Police Department so she

asked if she could make a few calls and see if she could get any information on the theft. Tiffanie called back Thursday morning and said that the owner of both businesses had not filed a police report so until they did she shouldn't worry. That phone call put Vita at ease because she knew the stolen money had to be illegal otherwise the owner would have reported the theft to the cops, but they didn't. And if they really thought a superhero stole it, were they stupid enough to come after her after seeing how she put a hole in a steel safe? Vita didn't think so but she had a bigger problem to deal with. Who was impersonating her and how were they able to jump the fence and put a hole in the safe the way they did. The only way she would have been able to do that would be after or during her transformation. She was stumped. How did someone pull it off and who?

THREE TO TANGO

Before dawn on Monday morning Kristen was on the way to Toni's house. They hadn't spoken in days and her gut was insisting Toni was up to something. Kristen couldn't believe she had trusted this hood rat to find out if Vita was the superhero. And besides that, she had confided in the skank that she and Vita had dated years prior and how she had gotten her heart broken by Vita. But lately Toni had been distant and unreachable. Kristen got the feeling the girl was hiding something the way she was so short on the phone and always hurrying off and seeming uninterested in any of their conversations.

Kristen parked around the corner again and seeing Toni's car parked in the driveway, decided to peak into the windows again just to be sure who all was home; company would be bad. She tip-toed to the back yard and peeked into Toni's bedroom window. She could see Toni was still asleep and alone but it was what Kristen saw all over Toni's bedroom floor that knocked her backward and onto the barbeque grill. She knocked the top off the grill and it fell onto the paved patio section with a loud thud. She quickly got up and ran, made it to her car and just sat there, still amazed at what she had seen.

Hearing the noise outside her bedroom window, Toni woke up and looked out but didn't see anything or anyone. She put on some sweats, a robe and slippers and walked outside to look around. She did see the top of the barbeque grill on the ground but thought maybe a cat or squirrel or something had knocked it off. She replaced it, walked around the rest of the duplex and not seeing anything suspicious, went back in the house. When she got back to her bedroom she realized she had left one of the blinds partly open and if anyone was looking through her window, they got a clear view of the money on her bedroom floor. Spooked that someone may be watching her, she quickly dressed, put all the money, less ten thousand dollars, back into the duffle bag, shoved the duffle bag into the trunk of her car and drove to a storage unit.

A new storage facility had just been built at the corner of DeKalb Avenue and Boulevard Street and she had grabbed a unit as soon as it opened. It was close by so as long as she made it there without being stopped by the police, she'd be okay.

Toni breathed a sigh of relief when she got there and quickly opened her storage unit and hid the duffle bag amongst the other items in there. She was unsure about leaving so much money in there but she didn't have another choice. She needed to stash it and keep a low profile until the public got tired of the news story. She'd go back to her normal routine of dating and spending time with Vita, making up with crazy, psycho Kristen and seeing her two men clients. She didn't have a short term agenda for the money, she was just happy to have it. She wasn't even sure what she was going to with the ten thousand she kept, she just liked the freedom she felt knowing she had it. Maybe she and Vita could go on a weekend vacation to Mexico or to the Bahamas or something nice and hot. She'd ask when they got together next.

Kristen hadn't left Toni's neighborhood and followed her. She stayed far enough away once inside the storage lot to make sure Toni didn't see her and peeped around the corner to try and see the storage unit number Toni was using. Luckily for her it was very easy to spot because another family was nearby her unit moving a carload of items into their unit and were still at it after Toni left. Kristen walked past, making note of Toni's number and pretended to be searching for her own storage locker.

When Toni returned home, she laid on
the couch. It was early and Toni knew
she'd probably wake Vita up if she called
but called anyway. The phone rang five
times before Vita finally answered.
"Good morning sleepy head," Toni said
in an early morning, sexy voice. She
could feel Vita smiling over the phone
and she was glad she had called.

"Hello stranger," Vita said trying
to sound sexy but her true *just woke up
from a deep sleep* voice was what came
through. "Haven't spoken to you in a
while," Vita said.

"I know," Toni replied. "I've been
watching the news and figured you had a
lot going on with the cops and the news
people so I thought I'd give you a few
days until things calmed down for you."

Vita was silent. *What a lame
excuse. We have been seeing each other
for weeks now, every day and every
night and in my time of need you
disappear? What happened to the girl
that swooped in, took us to a beautiful
cottage in Tennessee for a few days
when these troubles first started?* It was

like she was dealing with two different people and not sure which one she could trust.

"So what have you been up to?" Vita asked trying to hide her confusion. "I thought I'd hear from you sooner since you saved me last time I was in this same sort of mess."

"I know and I'm sorry, sweetie," Toni said. Vita smiled. She liked it when Toni called her sweetie. "So what do you have going on this week?" Toni casually asked purposely not answering the question and changing the subject. "I wanted to take you away for a weekend to maybe Mexico or somewhere fun and hot."

Vita didn't answer right away because it suddenly dawned on her that she couldn't remember what Toni said she did for a living. *How can she afford to take me away on a weekend trip with no legitimate source of income?*

Suddenly Toni heard a knock at her door at the same time her cell phone started to vibrate. "Let me call you right back," Toni said to Vita. "The post lady is here with a delivery."

"Ok," Vita replied, hanging up to the dial tone on the other end of the phone.

Toni reluctantly answered the phone after seeing Kristen's car parked outside her house. "Hello Kristen!"

"Hello Miss Lady," Kristen said. "I know it's early, but I was up and about early and realized I was near your neighborhood so I decided to stop by."

"What are you doing near my neighborhood this time of the morning?" Toni asked, getting more annoyed by the minute. "It's not even nine o'clock."

"I know but I was in the area and we haven't seen each other in a while. I was thinking of you while I was on this side of town and decided to stop by. Are you busy? Did I catch you at a bad time? Or do you have company?"

"None of the above," Toni said not trying to hide her annoyance. She was so sick of Kristen and sorry she ever met her. The only good thing that came out of ever knowing her was that she met Vita. That was it. Other than that, she brought no added value to her life. Awkwardly standing on Toni's front porch, Kristen said, "So are you going to let me in? I'm standing on your front porch looking like an idiot."

"I'll be right there," Toni said. She changed into a pair of sweats and a hooded sweatshirt, walked to the front door and let Kristen in. "Want some coffee?" Toni asked realizing she was probably up for the day. She walked into the kitchen and began making the coffee when suddenly she felt a sharp, electric shock running through her entire body.

It all happened so fast and before she could react, she was writhing on the floor, moving in spasms. *What the fuck?* she thought but couldn't do anything to stop what was happening. When she regained consciousness, the spasms had stopped and she looked up from the kitchen floor to see Kristen standing over her with a Taser.

Kristen helped Toni to her feet and sat her in a kitchen chair. That's when Toni realized that her hands were handcuffed behind her back. Realizing this was a very serious situation; she sat quietly and watched Kristen pace back and forth seeming to be calculating her next move.

"I knew you couldn't be trusted," Kristen began. "You think I'm an idiot, don't you?"

Toni didn't speak. Kristen was in her face screaming at her about how she betrayed her, how she used her for drinks, dinners and hanging out when they first met. "You were supposed to help me find out if Vita was the superhero but what did you do? You took my money and gave me shit! I could have gotten more information on my own," she screamed. "And I know you're fucking her!"

Toni met her crazy gaze when she said that. "Oh, that got your attention huh? You didn't know that I knew about that did you? My friends have been telling me for weeks that they've seen the two of you out, holding hands, looking all lovey dovey." Toni smirked a little after that tirade and when Kristen saw it, she slapped Toni hard across the face.

"So where did you get that money," Kristen said calmly. Toni didn't answer. "Maybe you didn't hear me so I'll ask you again. Where the fuck did you get the money?" Again Toni didn't answer and again Kristen slapped her hard across the face, this time knocking her to the floor.

It was then that Toni became scared. *This bitch is crazy, really crazy.* With Toni on the floor, Kristen kicked her in her back. Toni screamed. Kristen walked away and came back with an old phonebook. "I didn't know people still had these," she said. Kristen helped Toni back into the chair, then held the phonebook in both hands and slammed it down on Toni's head, knocking her back onto the floor.

Vita was still in bed waiting for Toni's call when she felt that familiar itch on her stomach. *Not now,* she thought. The timing couldn't have been worse. She wanted to stay out of sight until this robbery thing settled down but unfortunately she had no control over when she would be summoned to help someone. She jumped out of bed as the feeling became stronger, transformed into Vita The Superhero and took off from the rooftop. As she flew over the city, nothing was obvious; no fires, no large traffic accidents, no crowds of people, no smoke … no nothing.

Not sure where she was being taken, she let the powers guide her and to her surprise she landed in Toni's backyard. Before going in she looked through the kitchen window and was shocked by what she saw. Toni had Kristen by the throat and was holding her up with one hand, feet dangling in the air. And it looked like she had a broken pair of handcuffs around her wrists.

Not knowing what danger she was walking into, Vita turned the back door doorknob and walked in. Startled, Toni let Kristen go and she fell hard to the floor. Everything that happened next seemed to happen in slow motion to Vita. She saw Toni dressed in a similar outfit to what she had on and what she saw was exactly what she thought— broken handcuffs. Both women had bloody faces, cuts and bruises like they had been in a fierce brawl. And this was Vita's first time seeing Kristen in person since Chicago. She had seen them together in that picture Tiffanie had showed her and that was it.

The kitchen looked as if they had been fighting for a while but what Vita didn't see was anything Toni could have used to cut the handcuffs and that's when everything became crystal clear. It was her! Toni had captured some of Vita's superpowers through sexual contact and had figured out a way to store some of the powers and impersonate her and had stolen that money! What seemed like minutes to Vita was only a few seconds and the three women stood in silence staring at each other.

Kristen spoke first and directed her words towards Vita. "How does it feel? You thought you were all in love and shit not knowing you were just being used! Does it hurt? *Humm*? I hope it hurts as much as you hurt me when you rejected me years ago! I was in love with you and you just tossed me aside like I was nothing!"

Vita heard Kristin talking but she wasn't listening. During these initial seconds, she realized she had been played and her stomach flopped. She felt it rise up, turn over and fall back down. And at the same time it felt like her heart had been ripped from her chest, stomped on and put back. She was staring at Toni, not believing what was happening. *Did she ever love me?*

Toni walked towards her. Although Kristen was with them in the kitchen, it felt to Vita that she and Toni were the only two people in the room. "I can explain," Toni said. "This isn't what it looks like!"

"How is this not what it looks like?" Vita asked. "You look like me and by the looks of those broken handcuffs on your wrists; you have some of the same powers I have. How did you do it?" Vita asked.

"I don't know," Toni said. "I think it was through having sex with you but I'm not sure."

"Don't believe her," Kristen yelled from the other side of the kitchen. "She's got one vial of blood in her refrigerator and if she didn't knock you out and extract if from your body, then she took if from her own body after one of your fuck fests! She had two vials but used one to steal the money! She dressed up like you, stole the money and hid it in a storage locker at that new storage place on the corner of Boulevard and Dekalb Ave. Storage locker number 908. It's all there in a black duffle bag. She set you up to take the fall."

"Don't believe anything she's saying," Toni said calmly. "She's lying through her teeth!"

Vita looked towards the refrigerator but before she could take one step forward, Toni flew across the kitchen and stood in front of it, blocking it.

"She's been using you the whole time," Kristen continued yelling. "I paid her to get close to you and find out if you were the superhero! And she made secret recordings of you and let me hear them! This whole time, she's been playing you for a fool! And did you know she's been fucking me too and two guys who pay her for sex?"

With that last comment, Toni flew from the refrigerator to where Kristen was standing, grabbed her again with one hand and slammed her head against the kitchen cabinets until Kristen passed out. Vita didn't move. She was in shock.

So everything Toni told Vita was a lie. She really didn't love her, she was just using her. Toni was nothing but an opportunist looking out for herself and a whore from what Kristen said. Vita's mind was racing; she didn't know what to believe or whom to believe. She couldn't believe she could be so wrong about a person she loved. She really thought they had a future together and was sick to her stomach thinking of how she had been lied to. Momentarily snapping back to reality, Vita flew over to the refrigerator and ripped the door off its hinges and threw it across the room. She threw out everything that was inside but found no vials of blood.

Seizing an opportunity to try and get Vita to believe her side of the story, Toni said, "I told you there are no blood vials. I wouldn't do something that devious and underhanded to you. I love you Vita!"

Vita was confused. She wanted to believe Toni but something in her told her she was lying. If there was a blood vial it had to be somewhere in the house and probably in her bedroom. Vita took a few steps toward the bedroom when she noticed a potato that had rolled underneath the kitchen table. There was something strange looking about it so she reached underneath the table and picked it up. She saw a carved out hole in it and looking more closely at the floor where the potato had fallen, she saw it. A blood vial.

Toni saw Vita looking at the blood vial. As Vita bent down to pick it up, Toni jumped her and they began fighting. The madder Vita got, the stronger she got. But as strong as she was, Toni matched her strength. They threw each other through walls, broke furniture, smashed the sink in the bathroom and finally broke through the front door and landed in the front yard. They continued fighting until they saw the neighbors videoing them and taking pictures with their phones. Realizing Kristen had blurted out where the money was, Toni stopped fighting Vita and shot into the air, flying towards the storage unit. Vita followed, caught up with Toni and they started fighting in the air. By this time, news outlets sent reporters who were awestruck catching each unbelievable display of superhuman strength as they fought in the air.

Toni arrived at the storage unit seconds before Vita. She punched a large hole in the storage door and grabbed the duffle bag with the money in it but before she could fly away, Vita caught her and knocked her back into the storage unit, putting a large hole in the back wall. Toni tried to escape through the hole in the back wall but Vita pulled her back, slammed her on the cement floor and began choking her. Toni struggled to breathe, her arms and legs flailing about but Vita didn't stop. She was overcome with emotion over the hurt Toni had caused her, the lies she told and she was mad at herself for how she had opened herself up, let her guard down and for becoming vulnerable to a woman she believed loved her. The hard truth was that Toni only wanted to be with her because she was the superhero. And the thought of Toni impersonating her, almost sending her to jail and putting her life in danger, made her squeeze harder. Before she realized it, Toni was losing consciousness and close to death. Vita looked up and lots of people had gathered around the storage unit. She then realized she was being videoed attempting to kill someone. She let go of Toni's neck and realized Toni had changed back to her normal self. But she was lifeless. Scared to death Vita grabbed the bag of money and flew away.

Knowing she would be wanted by the police and sensing the media was already camped out at her apartment, Vita hid out at an elderly couple's home whom she looked after from time to time. She knew they were out of town visiting their daughter and grandkids so she used the spare key and let herself in.

She'd hide out here until she figured out what she was going to do next. Vita called Dillon from the couple's landline and left him a message, letting him know where she was. She was sure everyone had seen the video of the fight by now and was sure her friends were worried about her. She had dumped her cell phone somewhere when she fled the scene at the storage unit so she couldn't return the calls or text messages she was sure everyone was sending.

Vita waited until dark before she snuck into her apartment. She used a secret side entrance reserved for deliveries and building management. She grabbed anything she could fit into a few boxes and two large duffle bags but most of her things she had to leave behind. She made sure she took all of her personal items: pictures, cards, sex toys, electronics and as many clothes as she could fit in the bags. Before she left her apartment for good, she paused and took a long look around. She'd had fun in this apartment and she knew this was the last time she'd be in it so she stood for a while and took it all in. She felt sad that she had to leave her furniture, her kitchen gear, all of her cute stuff in the bathroom where she spent many relaxing nights in the tub but she had no choice, she couldn't stay.

Vita returned to the elderly couple's home where she continued to plan her next moves. She knew Dillon was deejay'ing an early private party that night at STK on Peachtree Street in Midtown so she made her way there and waited for him so they could talk. When he arrived he started taking his equipment out of his car but stopped when he saw her. Vita could see the sign of relief in his eyes that she was okay. They hugged and Dillon told her how he had to turn his phone off because of all the calls from the television shows, news channels and all his friends calling him.

"My voicemail keeps getting filled up within minutes," Dillon said. "I keep deleting them, but they keep calling."

Vita apologized and told Dillon where she was staying. "I might be leaving for a while," she said. "But I'm not sure yet. Whatever happens, I'll keep in touch. I promise!" Dillon nodded. "If you know someone who wants the apartment, they can have it. I'm not going back there but if you don't get someone in there the landlord will realize I'm gone when I don't pay the rent. I can't afford it anymore anyway." They talked a little more, hugged again and then Vita left.

Vita had another stop to make. She needed to speak with Kristen and get the truth about her relationship with

Toni. Kristen mentioned that she was staying at the W Hotel during her rant and assault at Toni's house. Vita wasn't sure which W Hotel so she decided to play this straight and call her and ask if they could meet. Kristen still had the same number and to Vita's surprise, Kristen agreed to meet and invited Vita to her suite at the hotel. This was not something Vita wanted to do with Kristen but she wanted to get the truth about what she knew about Toni. She was nervous getting off the elevator and almost turned around and left but she didn't. It was important to know the truth even if she didn't like what she was going to hear.

Kristen answered the door dressed in a short, tight dress and knee high boots. *Obviously she's confused about the nature of this visit.*

"Nice place," she said as she walked in. Kristen offered her something to drink but Vita declined, thinking Kristen might try to drug or poison her. "No thanks! I don't have a lot of time but I wanted to talk to you about Toni. I just want know how you met and what the nature of your relationship is."

Kristen seemed disappointed that Vita was only there to talk about Toni. "What about her?" Kristen said already annoyed that she had agreed to this meeting. "So the only reason you're here is to talk about Toni?"

Vita nodded. They sat down, Vita being sure to sit facing Kristen since she was crazy.

"So you want to know the truth about your love, Toni?" Again, Vita nodded yes. "Well she's not who you think she is," Kristen began. She went on to tell Vita she saw the first newscast of a woman superhero who lifted the car off those men and saved their lives. She said the woman looked so much like her that she came to Atlanta to find out. Kristen said her original plan was to hire a private detective to follow and gather info on her but then she met Toni at a party, told her about it and hired her.

"Her job at first was to find out as much as she could about you. That was it. But I could tell from the first time she reported back that she had accidently, on purpose, ran into you at the coffee shop, that she was attracted to you. And then she stopped recording you altogether and basically quit the job!"

Vita looked up at Kristen when she heard the word recording. "She was really recording me?" Vita asked Kristen. She had looked directly at Kristen when she asked her question and could see the look of satisfaction in that sour face. It was as if Kristen was enjoying the hurtful look on Vita's face.

"Yeah she was and I can prove it."
Kristen walked into the bedroom and
brought back a small recorder. She sat
the recorder on the coffee table and
pressed play. Vita heard Kristen and
Toni discussing whether or not Vita
could be the superhero. And she heard
Toni asking when she was getting paid.
Suddenly Vita felt that nauseous feeling
in her stomach again but this time she
felt like she was going to be sick.

Sensing her uneasiness, Kristen
pressed on. "And she has two guys she
fucks regularly and they give her money
and pay her rent. She stole the money
from one of their cousins and dressed
like you so everyone would think you did
it." Kristen continued telling Vita how
much she paid her overall and was sure
to tell her that the two of them were
sleeping together.

Vita had heard enough. She had
to get out of there. Kristen got drunk
while telling these tales and Vita wasn't
sure how much was the truth and how
much was embellishment. She stood up,
thanked Kristen and told her she wanted
to hear more but they'd have to do it
another time. Vita said she'd call her in a
day or two. And as she was saying it, she
knew she hoped she'd never see Kristen
again. She took a minute and took a last
look at someone who once was her
friend and coworker.

The woman hadn't changed much, her skin had more of a tannish glow to it being in California and she had cut her hair short and added highlights which brought out the blue in her eyes and her natural sandy colored hair color. She was a small, sexy woman but as Vita always thought, just not her type.

Once at the door, Vita stopped. "I need to ask you something. Where you the one who punched me in the head while I was dancing at The Harlem Bar one night and flattened my tire and busted out my car window? Was all of that you?"

Kristen was drunk so she told the truth. "Yeah, all of that was me. I wanted to get back at you for how you treated me."

Vita just shook her head. She always thought it was Kristen and now she knew for sure.

When she was back at the old couple's house, Vita played the recording on the voice recorder she took from Kristen. No doubt it was Toni's voice and before she could stop the hurt feeling that seemed to come out of nowhere, the first tear rolled down her cheek, followed by another and another. Tired and emotionally exhausted, she grabbed a comforter from the linen closet and lay on the couch. She tried to stop her mind from racing but she couldn't. She kept playing back all the things Kristen had said about Toni and she couldn't shake the sick feeling that came over her each time she thought about how she had been played for a fool and had fallen for a woman who was not the person she portrayed herself to be. *How did I not see it? How could I have been so naive?* And then her thoughts turned to people like Toni and how they could be so cruel, self-centered and selfish. Vita's last thoughts before she fell asleep were of Toni and if she ever really loved her.

In the morning, against her better judgment, she went to the hospital to see Toni to give her an opportunity to explain. She watched a news clip which showed the hospital where Toni was, so she headed there. Maybe Kristen was lying. Maybe she wasn't being completely truthful. She knew her reasoning was purely out of love but her heart was making the decisions right now.

Vita had to use wits and patience to get onto Toni's floor without being seen. Just like her apartment building, the media was all over, hovering like a pack of wild animals. When Toni was alone in her room, that's when Vita entered. Toni's eyes were blood red from almost being choked to death, pins were in her left leg and it was elevated and in a sling. Vita could see dark marks on her throat, marks that she had put there while trying to choke the life out of her. Toni tried to speak but Vita stopped her.

"The only thing I'm here for is the truth. Did you dress up like me and steal the money from that drug dealer?"

Toni nodded yes.

"Did Kristen hire you to meet me and find out if I was the superhero?"

Again Toni nodded yes.

"Are you having sex with two guys for money, like a prostitute?"

Toni shook her head no and mouthed the words, "No, no, no. I promise you no!"

Vita wanted to believe her so bad. She wanted to believe in the fairytale but she knew Toni was lying. She felt the tears resting on the bottom lids of her eyes and she was trying her best to keep them there.

Two nurses entered Toni's room and asked Vita how she got in and told her she had to leave, that visiting hours didn't start until the afternoon. Vita started to leave when Toni grabbed her hand and mouthed the words, "I love you!"

At that, the tears rolled down Vita's cheeks. She stepped aside so the nurses could work on Toni but before she left she placed the recorder on

Toni's side table. And it was queued to
the spot where Toni was telling Kristen
how she was going to get Vita to fall in
love with her and see where that would
get them. "If she is the superhero, it
could be financially beneficial for both of
us." And the recording had picked up
their toast, their laughter and their
kisses.

Vita returned to the house where
she was staying and packed her things.
She made sure everything was as it was
when she got there and left the elderly
couple a note explaining how she was
going away for a while but would be in
touch. She booked a private jet from
Embraer Executive Jets to Brazil leaving
in a few hours and reserved a car to pick
her up to take her from the airport. A
woman Vita had worked with at her last
job lived there and ran a predictive
dialer company. She was always inviting
Vita to come visit and there was no
better time than now.

The driver picked Vita up at three
o'clock on the dot. He placed her things
in the car but Vita carried the duffle bag
with the cash herself. She had the driver
make one stop before going to the
airport ... the hospital. She had him park
in the parking lot and took one last look
up at Toni's hospital room window. For
a minute she thought about running up
to her room and asking her to come with

her but her mind was in control now and her mind said no. As much as she loved Toni, Vita needed to leave, to go somewhere new and get a fresh start. She wasn't sure when and if she and Toni would ever see each other again but for right now the best move was to leave.

And with those thoughts and her heart in her hand, she told the driver she was ready and left it all behind.

THE END

Thank you for reading Unexpected Power! Please leave a review on Amazon or Barnes & Noble and you can check out other titles from Brigitte Marshall and more at: www.Printhousebooks.com

PRINTHOUSE BOOKS

Read it, Enjoy it, Tell a friend.

VIP INK Publishing Group, Incorporated.
Atlanta, GA.

www.PrintHouseBooks.com